THE CHRONICLES OF HADLEE SHEEP

Susan Harrison

MINERVA PRESS

LONDON

MONTREUX   LOS ANGELES   SYDNEY

THE CHRONICLES OF HADLEE SHEEP
Copyright © Susan Harrison 1997

ISBN 1 86106 315 6

First Published 1997 by
MINERVA PRESS
195 Knightsbridge
London SW7 1RE

Printed in Great Britain by
BWD Ltd, Northolt, Middlesex

THE CHRONICLES OF HADLEE SHEEP

To Christy, from Mummy – with love, and to my father, Harry Dewing, who first told me stories of Gilbert and his cohorts

About the Author

Susan Harrison lives in a Cotswold stone cottage in rural Wiltshire with her husband Phillip and son Christopher.

The cottage is set in rolling countryside running down to the River Marden where she walks the springer spaniel Tealeaf and Bramble the terrier(ist). Kiwi, Christopher's cat, and Mellors and Mackeson the ferrets complete the menagerie.

She enjoys music, gardening, organising the annual village pig-roast, watching her son play cricket and football... and shopping in nearby Bath!

On holiday in Malta in 1995, she decided to write a short story to amuse Christopher, then eight years old.

The chapters, featuring not only his favourite toy animals, one as old as himself, but friends and characters from their village, sort of grew into a book.

The result, you hold in your hand...

Dramatis Personae

Hadlee Sheep	*Narrator, novelist, author of* Malteser Merino *and superstar sheep*
Embers the Dragon	*His chum: aviator, inventor, bicyclist and fire hazard*
Sir Richard Branson	*Another aviator*
Runcie	*A monkey*
Edward	*A Southampton bear*
Ernie	*A resident of 'Sesame Street'*
The Young Master	*The toys' 'minder' and owner of*
Cuddly	*A precious piece of cloth with one very dirty corner*
Badminton Bounce Hayzee the Horse Moley the Mole	*Three toys known as 'The Andrews Sisters' fond of singing in three-part harmony*

Wackett and Birch	*Teachers at 'Derry Hill' the Young Master's school*
Millie Molly Manly	*The Young Master's music teacher*
HRH Queen Elizabeth	
The Queen Mother	*Embers' chum*
Kevin Iles	*A local cricket hero*
Rosler Rustler Mayzee Pip	*Hayzee's relations from the New Forest*
Russ	*A piano-playing seal*
Gypsy Rose Madder	*A fortune teller who, in a certain light, resembles a dragon of Hadlee's acquaintance*
Miss Tarragon	*Hadlee Sheep's agent*
A Canada Goose Mr Toad Ratty	*Friends encountered on a Thames riverbank*
Coley	*Moley's brother*

Bramble and Tealeaf	*The Young Master's terrier and springer spaniel*
An Anonymous Chicken	
Kiwi	*The Young Master's cat*
Squirry	*A squirrel with an annoying squeak*
Hipi	*A coathanger*
Columbus Killaire Wattie	*Donkeys: Badminton Bounce's brothers*
Gilbert 'Mr Gollivator'	*A keep-fit fanatic, entertainer and erstwhile magician*
Squiggles	*A bear with an aeroplane called* Liberty Belle

Encountering Embers

My first memory is of an unceremonious trip to Harvey Nichols in Knightsbridge – at least I started out with a good address – and life on the shelf in their 'soft toy' department, alongside the hobby horses, pedal cars and junior bicycles.

After closing time my colleagues and I would scamper down and race the pedal cars round the counter, hold 'hobby horse' Derbies and, for a bit of relaxation (it can be very boring for a sheep on a shelf all day), read stories like *Winnie-the-Pooh*, *Old Bear* and *Paddington*. I dreamed of adventure and wondered why only bears wrote books!

One day, a young lady with an infectious giggle came into the shop and the next thing I knew, I was off the shelf and being scrutinised for safety! What a (mint) sauce. It seemed she was concerned that there was nothing about me that could harm a 'Christopher' – whatever that was. Safe as houses me, I could have told her if she'd had the civility to ask, although I must admit my tail has spent the last five years in a sock drawer.

I was whisked off, and presented to this 'Christopher' who did nothing interesting at all except (with a little help) christen me 'Hadlee' after the New Zealand cricketer Sir Richard. Good choice – I liked cricket, had bowled the odd Sindy maiden over back at the shop and batted a bit as well, even faced those fearsome felt kangaroos Thomson and Lillie without disgrace and I once bowled Khan the tiger out for a (toy) duck.

I was placed in the boy's cot with a monkey called 'Runcie', a bear known as 'Edward' (isn't there always a bear?), rather haughty and serious – a senior sort of citizen from Southampton who was inclined to start each sentence with "we Southampton bears..." (what a yawn) – and an All-American whizz-kid by the name of 'Ernie' who was into striped jumpers and had a friend who lived in Sesame Street called 'Bert'. He promised to be a bit of fun. We were all studiously ignored by our Young Master, who preferred to carry round with him a bit of old cloth called 'cuddly'.

A sheep with my talents needs a challenge and during this time I envisaged a plan that one day I would be famous! I'd hit the headlines in all the right places... perhaps I'd be the second Richard Branson... 'Sir Hadlee Sheep' has a certain ring, don't you think? *Fleece Atlantic*, *Fleece Flyer*, *Fleece Phonographs*.

You name it, I could do it, confident old sheep even then... if only I could let the side of the cot down to reach the phone. Memo: mobile phone essential.

Nineteen ninety-two saw me dusted down for a holiday in North Wales with 'cuddly' (what else?) and a game of Monopoly. My sort of entertainment, Monopoly: Ernie and I played it under cover of the duvet, I already had six hotels in Mayfair and made Euston a no-go station for Thomas the Tank Engine.

During our holiday, between showers, there sauntered into my life a scarlet and green glove puppet – a (very)

Welsh dragon known as 'Embers'. He hummed *Cwym Rhondda* and I could quite see why those Saxons had it in for the Welsh: "No surrender, no retreating! Harlech wins the fight!" indeed. (The Young Master is learning this, and other tunes, on his keyboard.)

This rather eccentric piece of egotistical Welshness soon muscled his way into our game of Monopoly. He is very keen on orienteering, travel and waving. A real daredevil, a high-flyer and a perfect pain to boot (preferably over a fence to practise his flying). His ambition was, and still is, to form his own airline – *Dragon Air* – and he (of course) would be his own trademark – Dragon Rampant!

His passion for underwater swimming was put to the test when he inadvertently set foot in the washing machine with a set of bedclothes. I still remember him waving happily as he sped past the glass door whilst others asked, "Why (and thank heavens) are red glove puppets colourfast when M&S knickers aren't?" Memo: please remember that I, myself, have an allergy to washing powder and would never be caught napping at the launderette...

I digress: working on the old maxim, 'if you can't beat them, join them', the red menace and I joined forces on the plan for a great adventure. I also decided to record our antics in a diary. What's good enough for Samuel Pepys is okay by me, and with the demon dragon around, the 'Great Fire' could be more than just a page in a history book.

The Young Master and his family were planning a holiday in Malta: this could be our chance for an escapade of a lifetime. We timed it well – just as they were ready to leave, we stowed away (as I expect Richard Branson did as a boy): we dived into an overnight bag, re-zipped it, and I stuck a damp sock in Embers' mouth... just to be on the safe side!

Malteser Merino

After a good deal of swinging about, the bag, now suitably inscribed 'KM 10885, Destination Malta', was set down. The Young Master's hand felt inside the bag and pulled out the camera. Help – Embers had just finished the film, he'd found a hole in a seam and had snapped everything that passed.

The hand again, this time it grabbed our red rover by the tail and to cries of "how did he get in there?" Embers disappeared, waving as he went.

I coughed discreetly. The Young Master dived back into the bag, carefully lifted me out and hugged me... he even allowed me to sit in his seat (with cuddly) on the aeroplane and look out of the window.

Back in the bag, Embers, with paperbacks, football statistic charts, bottles of sun tan lotion and insect repellent for travelling companions, was placed on rollers (he'd always wanted to learn to skate!) and whisked off to the cargo hold. Still waving, his little red hand slowly vanished from sight. Would I ever see my carmine companion again?

It seems you can't keep a good dragon down and en route to the plane he managed to visit Air Traffic Control and divert one flight to Heathrow and turn another one back to Peru. He slipped back into his travelling bag and out again when he reached the 'apron' and succeeded in sabotaging (he wanted to know how it worked!) our 737 engine, ensuring a two hour delay. Not bad for a novice?

I began to think that this was the life for me! The stewardesses were charming, and we had a most amusing game of pass-the-parcel with a young traveller called Adrien... unfortunately I was the parcel, but I was invited onto the flight-deck (the Young Master accompanied me) and I made a few notes for 'future reference'.

At the hotel Embers and I were reunited and jumped under the Young Master's bedclothes for a good night's sleep. Tomorrow we would explore!

We slipped out and scampered down the road. We bought Ernie a baseball cap for his collection, Runcie a banana-shaped pencil case and Edward a wallet for his pension book (ho-ho!). We found the sea and had a paddle. "Let's hire some bicycles," enthused Embers, a keen bicyclist, and we did.

An hour later, having encountered roundabouts, one way systems and bumps in the road worthy of a big dipper, the Red Flash was a gibbering wreck. Back to the hotel for a mint julep.

Tomorrow we'd take the bus.

The one we chose was heading for the ferry to Gozo... isn't that a Muppet?

See a sign on a lorry – 'Sultana Brothers' – and decide to adopt the name and travel incognito with false beards and sunglasses, in case Mr Branson is about. On the ferry we met a Mr Brown; we asked him if he was the one related to Paddington. "Certainly not, young sheep," he replied. So much for the disguise.

We clambered onto a rickety old bus and shook, rattled and rolled round the island: sightseeing.

Lunch and postcards. Embers in his excitement sets fire to the corner of Ernie's card...he'll recognise the signature. Notice Mr Brown eating a sandwich: marmalade!!

The tour guide looks like Mary Poppins and she has taken a shine to Embers; lets him sit in the front seat, although she thinks he's a hippo (snigger). She tells us that they hold horse races down the High Street on a Sunday – Embers thinks that sounds fun – and we spot a 'Hotspurs' banner in a window. Perhaps that nice Sue Barker will be waiting round the corner to introduce *Grandstand*.

We post our cards. Just catch sight of the address on one Mr Brown is sending... Windsor Gardens. "Perhaps it's to the Queen Mother?" suggests Embers, who has a hankering for a royal crest on his notepaper.

In the evening we peep into the disco. It looks like more fun, Ernie would have loved the *Birdie Song* and, just for him, we put the left foot in, left foot out, in, out, in... you know the rest: knees bend, arms stretched, baah, baah, baah! We jived and boogied till bed time.

Next day: breakfast, and in a rush to get to the pool, Embers gets hiccups. A dragon with hiccups is not recommended, but a shot of foam from the fire extinguisher dampens most of the damage.

The hire car has arrived, Maltese style: no brakes. The Young Master is off to Valetta so we tag along. We sneak off to the fish market and find a boat. We knew we shouldn't but we couldn't resist it. We hopped in and set off to look at the Grand Harbour. Embers took the tiller and, overcome by the excitement, we find ourselves heading for a tanker 'amidships'. Memo: if his airline ever takes off, find another pilot!

Supper: Embers is saddened to learn that 'Coalite and Custard' is not the sweet of the day... we see a poster: 'Talent Competition'...

Next morning, by the pool, we decide on our routine. Will it be our close harmony, *Baah, Baaah, Baah, Baaah Baa-bra Anne*, or our Baah-Baah Shop Quartet? Perhaps not, there are only two of us. Embers suggests *Cwym Rhondda* (he always does) or *Puff the Magic Dragon*. Would we ever agree?

Embers is complaining of sunburn from under his knotted handkerchief. How can he tell? I pose with a mint julep for a photograph... talk about Baywatch, more like Baaawatch.

The disco, the talent competition, much nervousness and we're on! We have decided on a medley (memo: we really need a keyboard player). Embers does his best with the comb-and-paper, sets light to the paper and someone throws a bucket of water over him, I slide across the wet floor as Embers strikes up with *Thursday Night Fever* on the banjo, I skid back, trip and do a double somersault, grab the first thing that passes – Embers' tail – and we twirl frantically round the floor. Somehow we finish together, the spotlight is on us and the disc jockey hands us the trophy. Stars are born!

Time to go home: Embers is waving goodbye to the hotel (it doesn't wave back). Having decided to write about all our adventures in my diary, I am wondering if a short novel would be possible and determine to buy a laptop computer when I return home.

We've swapped addresses with Percy, a penguin from Penge (a pasa doble perfectionist with his penfriend Penelope), Boris, a budgie from Buggiba, and Denzil Duck from Dagenham and his sister Vera.

Embers spends the journey 'cabin class' making copious notes on how not to run an airline. Mr Brown is snoring in the seat behind us. That battered suitcase looks familiar, it has an 'I love Peru' sticker, but I just can't read his luggage label.

As we peep out from the hand baggage heading for passport control, who should whizz past us in a 'courtesy' buggy but Mr Brown. "If we'd travelled *Virgin* we'd be in that," murmurs Embers.

"Bet he is the one with the bear, there's always a bear lurking in a story somewhere." Just then a familiar felt hat appears in the arrivals lounge.

It's Not Quite Cricket

Resisting all efforts to get me into the washing machine for a post-holiday 'spin', I am settling back into our normal routine. Up on the Young Master's bed we tell our tale to Edward (thrilled with his pension book cover) and Ernie (ditto his cap) and three other friends known as 'the Andrews Sisters'. I should explain...

They are a motley trio of toys: 'Badminton Bounce' is a glove puppet and donkey of doubtful distinction. Named after the horse trials winner of 1994, he claims he can trace his ancestry (via Red Rum!) back to the Darley Arabian and also claims to have won the Grand National (several times), the Derby, The Queen Mother Champion Chase (Embers shakes his head – she'd never jump over those fences without losing her hat) and the four o'clock at Newton Abbot as well.

'Hayzee' is a pony from the New Forest with a love of nature and a passion for apples, rambling and Trivial Pursuits.

'Moley' the mole who always has his snout in the Young Master's encyclopedia and whose Virgin Atlantic filofax makes me highly suspicious, makes up the trio. They are 'the Andrews Sisters' because of their fondness for singing three-part harmony not because of their resemblance to Patti, Laverne and Maxine.

Embers, in a decline because he couldn't find the keys to any of the Jumbo Jets at Gatwick, is concentrating on The Tour de France... with those legs? He says travel broadens a dragon's mind, and who am I to disagree.

To my total surprise, that nice Sue McGregor has just said on the radio that there will be daily reports on the race, and the Andrews Sisters are tuning his bike... at the moment they have a little Wagner on Radio 3! The Red Flash is busy jogging round the block, humming *Dragons of Harlech* and doing time trials round the Pewsham roundabout. Traffic: chaos.

Having waylaid a packet of Maltesers (for the spelling) from a small child outside school, I can now send the draft manuscript of my first novel *Malteser Merino* to the publishers with confidence. Agatha Christie, Enid Blyton, Beatrix Potter... Winnie the who? Memo: practise the flourish on the signature for the book signings.

Friday: To Goatacre for the annual fête at the cricket club. Now, the Young Master fancies himself as a bit of a cricketer and, as you probably know, his hero is Alec Stewart. We threw the wellie, bought the raffle tickets and were tempted by the cake stall in the best of British traditions.

Edward was busy 'guessing the weight of the weasel' in the slips and at mid wicket, Ernie was 'guessing the number of sweets in the jar'. They both resisted 'pin the tail on the donkey' at cover point, in case Bounce found out!

At silly mid off, Gypsy Rose Madder (those little red ears look familiar?) will tell your fortune if you cross her

palm with silver, and the Heidi Hunt School of Dancing were Travolta-ing away with their *Grease Lightnin'* routine at third man.

I wandered over to the golf competition, run by a Freddy Mercury look-alike. "Aren't you Hadlee Sheep?" he enquired with some nervosity. I had to come clean (Persil-phobic though I am!) and say, yes, I was that very sheep. I asked him if his friend Montserrat Caballe had opened the fête only to discover he wasn't Freddy Mercury at all but Kevin Iles, the Captain of Goatacre's victorious side in the Village Cricket Championships at Lords in 1988.

Covered in confusion, I decided to beat a hasty retreat to the boundary and the coconut shy where the Young Master was knocking them in the 'Iles' with his accurate throwing technique. Coconut in hand we all trooped off to the 'novelty stall'.

'Name That Bear' the banner proclaimed.

"Easy – Teddy," says Edward. "Only us Southampton bears are called Edward."

"Sooty," says a little boy covered in candy floss.

"Paddington," adds his sister who, I note, is wearing yellow wellingtons.

"Aloysius," I chip in, casually.

"You've won, you've won!" says Mrs Iles senior, and plants a big sloppy kiss (what a mint sauce) on my cheek. I accept my prize graciously, and with a small bear tucked under my arm, we wander off to watch the Young Master 'Beat the Goalie', and goalie duly beaten and the chocolate prize received we head for home. Not for us the bicycle: why wobble on two wheels when you can have four? That's my motto!

But, bicycles seem to be this week's fashion accessory (NB, they can make a novel coffee table) and having set yet another trend, Embers has left for France. Miss McGregor has not mentioned 'The Red Flash' yet so I can only assume he's so far in the lead, they've missed him...

Embers has just faxed me from Dinan. He and Chris Boardman have stopped for a picnic near a plantation of Christmas trees. (Memo: could be a profit in Christmas trees – rabbits could be a nuisance.) They are about to start the arduous 223.5 kilometre stage to Lannion, hugging the coast at the mercy of the stiff sea breezes. (Isn't *The Times* informative? The breezes won't be the only things stiff.)

On With the Motley!

Monday: more cricket. The Young Master takes a turn in the nets to demonstrate his forward defensive, his wicket keeping, his catching and his rolling over twice and shouting 'howzat?' technique. He's obviously been studying his Geoff Boycott video, I can tell, but with a few pointers from me he could be a nice little all-rounder. All the running about makes him hungry and he devours a cheese and pickle sandwich.

Tuesday: tennis. Now, I'm no Andre Agassi (I'm better looking) and the Young Master's mum is no Wimbledon ballboy (or is that ballperson?), but I think my young man has the makings of a tennis player. We had no Tarango tantrums and since he had his hair 'sheared' the other day he even looks quite presentable. The final set, and he declared himself ready for yet another C&P sandwich. Memo: find new brand name for pickle, this one makes me nervous!

Wednesday: the Young Master tries his hand at hockey and is declared a natural. Time for a sandwich, not too much pickle.

Obviously having taken the lead from me, the lady of the house is thinking of writing a novel. She has decided to change the characters' names, in the traditional manner, to protect the not-so-innocent. She herself, on the Young Master's advice, will be 'Katie' and the Young Master,

'Jamie'. I've emmm... tinkered with the plot, just slightly... with my literary leanings, she'll probably appreciate my help...

Bounce will portray 'Burmese' – the Queen's favourite horse. Hayzee will take the part of 'Devon Loch' (ouch!). Edward will portray King Edward VII as an old man (he's a natural for it) and Moley will take the cameo role of 'Mole'. Ernie (doubling on clapper-board) will play Princess Margaret, Embers the Queen Mother (it's the waving), Runcie, (the Primate of All England) The Archbishop of Canterbury, and I shall probably take the romantic lead.

The action starts on the patio: "Katie sat in her sun-drenched garden enjoying the last of the afternoon sun. Jamie was playing football with his friend, Ben... this half hour was her own... Suddenly, two bicycles swished down the hill. The Queen Mother, veiled hat askew, waved merrily as she freewheeled past the house but who was her mysterious companion. The obviously false beard concealed nothing, it could only be Hadlee Sheep...

Memo: perhaps the video business could be lucrative... must speak to Embers and Ernie – we'd look good on film. Second memo: has Branson hit the film industry yet? Find out.

No news from the Tour De France so Embers MUST still be in the lead (unless he's stopped to decorate all those Christmas trees!). Cycling is definitely the 'in' thing round here: the Andrews Sisters, out for a jaunt, have just bumped into the vicar's wife. Knowing Hayzee's steering I'm not surprised.

Saturday: the music lesson. I ought to explain that the Young Master's teacher, Mrs Manley, a sprightly septuagenarian who in the 1950s trod the boards with her own show-band (Millie Manley and The Milestones), lives in a Hansel and Gretel style thatched cottage with roses round the door, just past the postbox in the village. She can turn her hand to anything: ballroom dancing, swimming and playing the drums – the only thing she doesn't have time to do is make gingerbread!

I digress: Mrs Manley has decided to teach the Young Master, who till now has entertained us on the keyboard, to play the organ in a fortnight! All for the benefit (?) of the school production of *Joseph and his Technicolor Dreamcoat* (limited numbers of tickets available from Messrs Wackett & Birch, Derry Hill School). All this and a music exam on Tuesday! I do my best to encourage him, suggest *Baa-Baa Black Sheep* or *Baah, Baaah, Baah, Baaah Baa-bra Anne*. "Very nice, Mr Sheep, but the examiner is expecting *Rock Around the Clock* says Mrs Manley. And the Young Master spends the morning with scales, arpeggios, andantes and Rocking Around the Clock: one o'clock, two o'clock, time for the old C&P sandwich.

Arrive home to find Embers' 'Queen Mother' costume has arrived and Damon Hill in pole position for the Grand Prix. That debonair Desmond Lynham omits to mention Embers in his Tour De France report, although Alec Stewart gets a mention for a suspected broken finger.

Now, you might be wondering what the Andrews Sisters have been up to all this time: so am I. They've gone strangely quiet and it's a worry to a sheep. (Small joke there if you look hard enough.)

Egon Ronay says he will not have fish for supper thank you, he'll have another cheese and pickle sandwich. He didn't, but he didn't get the hoki either as this week's mystery is where has the fish gone? Empty fridge, empty freezer, peer down cat's throat – not a sign of it. Probably disappeared in the Studley Triangle which is just up the road near the postbox, on the way to Mrs Manley's house.

Tuesday: what a night. It did not surprise me yesterday afternoon when the Young Master asked me to accompany him again, to music. His arpeggios needed a little polishing before the big day tomorrow. His Doh-Ray-Me has Fah a long, long way to go. (Memo: we could do *The Sound of Music* – Embers would make a smashing nun and Edward could be Mother Superior.)

They were obviously so busy that the Young Master shot off home leaving me on the mantelpiece with a large clock, a selection of family photographs, a half-eaten sweet, three second class stamps and 40p in small change.

Around nine, I heard the telephone. Mrs Manley answered it and I heard her, in a questioning tone, ask, "Sheet? what sheet?... Oh sheep – no sheep here, you want Studley Farmhouse." I coughed discreetly. "That tatty thing! I was just going to put it with Christopher's Joseph music on the washing machine in the scullery. It'll be quite safe there." My mind was racing...

Scullery!... could be we do Cinderella at Christmas? Scullery! Washing machine; HELP!! I spent the night very quietly, hoping no one would creep down and put me on short spin. To amuse myself I found an old envelope and scribbled on the back: Cinderella... I wonder... We'll hire the village hall... Ol' green scales is a dead cert for Buttons... Dandini just 'is' Hayzee... Audition for the Ugly Sisters: bears only need apply.

Mice might be a problem (they always are in the village hall) but there's bound to be an odd pumpkin kicking about. Edward can play the king (there's always a king in a pantomime) and the Queen Mum can audition for the Fairy Godmother. I'll ask that nice Mr Lloyd Webber to write a few tunes, I'll play Prince Charming and I'll wear my coat with golden lining, bright colours shining, wonderful and new...

And in the East the dawn was breaking, the world was waking, any dream will do. On top of a washing machine any dream WILL DO! I missed the Young Master reading to me till way past his mother's cocoa hour and I was delighted to hear his footsteps as he arrived to collect me on his way to school. Perhaps I could give that teacher of his, Miss Brindley, a few pointers while I was there.

It's Embers' birthday in a fortnight and he's asked me to post the invitations. He fancied a party in a hot-air balloon – I advised against it. So we're just having a quiet little 'do' with a few friends; sizzle a sausage or two, marshmallows, that sort of thing.

I glance at the envelopes: The Young Master, Mr R. Branson, c/o Windsor Tea Rooms, Elizabeth Windsor, Windsor, The Second Battalion Royal Welsh Fusiliers, Windsor Barracks, Mrs Q. Mother Ret., Windsor, Mr P. Bear, Windsor Gardens (that I don't believe!). He must have negotiated a good price for a job lot of 'I love Windsor' keyrings for the party bags.

Hayzee: The Horse's Tale

Hayzee was a New Forest pony. He was dark chestnut with a wide white blaze, big black eyes and a flaxen mane. As a foal he lived at Furzey Lawn just to the north of the big town of Lyndhurst where the local people did their shopping and in the summer the tourists (grockles, his father called them) came to buy their postcards and souvenirs of their holiday. Many a young visitor would return home with a cuddly toy pony or a glove puppet just like Hayzee.

His twin brothers Rosler and Rustler were older than Hayzee, and they also had a sister, Mayzee, and a kid brother, Pip. They lived with their mother under a huge oak tree by a cricket pitch and spent many happy hours watching the humans scampering up and down all summer long, getting hot and tired and ready for the picnic waiting for them in the boot of their car. Now picnics were what the ponies liked best... especially apples.

Mayzee didn't go on 'boring' jaunts with her brothers, she would stay at home near the oak tree. She enjoyed being in the tourists' photographs. She would bat her long black eyelashes, cross her elegant fetlocks and pose. She often said that when she grew up she wanted to be a model and change her name to Raquel. The brothers would snigger and trot off to find adventure.

The ponies loved cricket (nearly as much as they loved apples and sugar lumps) and sometimes their Grandpa Oatz would take them across the Forest to Balmer Lawn or White Moor where all the important games were held. Once, at White Moor, Hampshire played Surrey and one of the Surrey team, called Alec Stewart, made a special fuss of the ponies. After tea he pulled out of his pockets sugar lumps! That was a treat. How Pip and Hayzee loved sugar lumps.

They followed the Hampshire results in the newspapers left behind by the tourists. Rustler said that one day he would have an adventure, he would go to Portsmouth to see Robin Smith bat. Then he would go to the Village Cricket Finals at Lords. Goatacre won that last year, he added importantly, they are from Wiltshire. Rosler said he would rather learn to bowl like Norman Cowans, then HE would be at Lords, bowling. Hayzee, who based his fielding technique on Derek Randall and his wicket keeping on HIS Mr Stewart, just loved the statistics, he now followed Surrey and could tell you who won what, and when. Mayzee checked the racing results – they worried about Mayzee!

The ponies treasured long walks. Hayzee knew all about the wildlife in the Forest – butterflies, grass snakes and frogs. He spotted nuthatches, hen harriers and wrens which to most of the visitors would remain unnoticed. Down by the River Bartley he had made friends with a kingfisher called Janesmoor, and a Dartford warbler called Maureen. Hayzee and Pip liked being down by the river best of all and sometimes they would take some apples, acorns and oatcakes tied up in red-spotted handkerchiefs and spend the whole day there.

Homeward bound once, by Lodgehill cottages, Hayzee and Pip saw two bicyclists. Nothing odd about that – there were people on bicycles all over the Forest in the summer, but these two were different: one was an elderly lady in a fancy hat (fancy that, thought Hayzee, some hat!) and the other (with a Welsh pennant on his handlebars) was a dragon!! They rushed home to tell their mum, who was busy scolding young Mayzee for flirting with a racehorse on his way home from a point-to-point at Fordingbridge.

On special days, such as birthdays, anniversaries and Mothering Sundays, Granny Smith who lived at Woodfidley, near Beaulieu, would pack a special picnic and they would all meet at the 'Knightwood Oak'. From Brockenhurst and Boldre, Bashly and Burley, the family would gather, play games, sing songs (Granny's Great Nephew would play the squeezebox and Uncle Nijinsky, a great Northern Dancer, would join in), and the foals would play 'Blind Pony's Buff' and bob for apples. They'd enjoy a feast of oatcakes, Bramley pie, acorn tarts and cider, and then Titas Oatz would play his fiddle.

On their way home in the twilight, Grandpa Oatz would take them through Perry Wood and tell them ghost stories. The trees would cast scary shadows and owls and bats would swoop to see who these strangers were. Mayzee would hold Cousin Shergar's arm tight. They would look through the windows of the Balmer Lawn hotel where the last of the cricketers would be telling tall stories in the bar or they'd go to Rhinefield House where there were always parties, music and dancing.

Some of Hayzee's best friends were the foxhounds which were kennelled near Furzey Lawn. When they went out on exercise Hayzee and Pip would play with them and trot along the wide rides swapping anecdotes and telling tales of Medyg and Heythrop Brimstone.

Occasionally, in the winter, they would go hunting with the hounds. Once at Bramshaw they stayed out all day. Hounds checked at Bramble Hill and Hayzee and Pip wandered a little way from the pack. They couldn't believe their eyes: they saw a toucan. It swooped down, introduced itself as 'Fred' (funny name for a toucan, thought the ponies) and asked it they had any soft fruit with them. A banana would do nicely. They did have an apple which they gave to the toucan who promised to come to tea, bringing peaches and plums and damsons, when he and his Uncle Guinness were flying over Furzey Lawn.

They liked him. He was a colourful chap and very friendly. He and his uncle lived in London. They were on holiday. Guinness was asleep at the moment on a nearby branch, his big yellow beak tucked under his wing. He'd been down to the local pub, The 'Crown and Stirrup', and imbibed rather too much of their fresh firkin of Ferret's Favourite. They laughed as they heard him snore: a bit of a perilous perch for an intoxicated toucan.

The Beaulieu Road sales were something they avoided. They'd heard tales of dark deeds, deals struck at midnight, gypsies and horse thieves. They knew one day they would all find new homes but their applejack days in the New Forest would always be special memories.

One day in the autumn, Hayzee, Rustler and Rosler went into Lyndhurst. There was a museum there which the ponies liked to visit. It told them the old ways of the Forest, showed them old fashioned things, like wagons and milk churns and scythes for making hay. It was as if the stories Grandpa Oatz recounted had come to life. His early days at Furzey Lawn were his favourite subject for a good yarn.

Mayzee and Pip were out collecting apples while their mum waved the older ponies goodbye.

"Remember," she said, "if you find a nice young master who'll take care of you, you and the young person have my blessing."

They trotted off and turned to wave as they reached the kennels.

"I couldn't leave here," said Rosler, "I'd be too sad."

"I'd like a bit of adventure," said Rustler, "I'd like to live on Dartmoor and play for the Minor Counties... before I go to Lords" (he remembered to add!).

They trotted on in companionable silence till they came to the museum. There were lots of visitors and one young boy had a sheep tucked under his arm. The boy put him down carefully to study a book on knots.

"He's joined the cubs," explained the sheep. "He's tying knots in everything, even the Red Menace's tail." (The sheep sniggered rather infectiously.) "Embers, that's my friend, is a dragon – he's always getting himself tied up in knots. What we really need is a book on how to untie them!"

"Do you know," the sheep continued, "that Embers will be at the Town Fayre this afternoon, he's busy now getting ready for it. He calls himself 'Gypsy Rose Madder', and he reads fortunes. Utter nonsense – he makes it up as he goes along – but the funny thing is, he always gets it right. Last month he saw spots and the Young Master caught chicken pox, and last week he predicted our Young Master would win a silver football medal, and he did! You should tag along with us, it would be great fun. I've another friend called Bounce –

you'd get on well with him, he love apples! My name's
Hadlee, by the way, I write books and create musicals."

Hayzee thought about it. It did sound like fun and this
Young Master seemed to be very kind. He was making a
fuss of all the animals in the museum, even the big horse
outside (it was really a man dressed up but Hayzee didn't
think he ought to spoil the joke).

"I'm going with Mr Sheep to the Town Fayre," he told
his brothers. "Tell mum I'll be back a bit late, will you."

At the Fayre there was lots to see and do. Hayzee and
Bounce bobbed for apples and won a football on the
tombola.

"The Young Master will love playing with that," said
Bounce to his new friend. "Shall we have a go on the
swings?"

And they did.

A 'celebrity guest' was going to judge the painting
competition which Hadlee, who considered himself just a
tad artistic, had entered.

Hayzee, with some nervosity, went to see Gypsy Rose
Madder. "I see a handsome dragon," she said, gazing
into her crystal ball. "You will go on a journey by car,
there will be singing, laughter and a strange squeak... and
a sheep will be celebrating too..."

At that moment the results of the painting competition
were announced. Third prize: Victoria Collins – as
Bounce and Hayzee made their way to the podium they
could hear a strange squeaking noise, Gypsy Rose Madder
had got that bit right – second prize: Jonathan Williams.
"The grand challenge cup – to be presented by our star
celebrity guest – for his delightful family portrait
'Swaledale Sheep at Emmerdale – Uncle Seth' first prize:
Mr Hadlee Sheep.

To loud applause Hadlee Sheep went up to collect his prize. No one cheered more than Hayzee who was having a wonderful time. Hadlee accepted the challenge cup, a huge rosette and a souvenir magic wand from none other than Sooty!

Muttering "mint sauce" Hadlee returned to his friends. Hayzee had enjoyed himself so much that he decided that if he was asked he would go home with the Young Master.

"Can't we take him with us?" he heard the boy ask his mum.

She said "No."

Hayzee was disappointed, but as the Young Master and Hadlee disappeared towards their car, she turned to Hayzee and invited him to jump into her handbag. He did, and when they were all in the car heading for their home in Wiltshire, he popped up.

"Surprise, surprise!" he shouted.

From the front seat (where he was giving directions – Dragon's Directions), the Dragon groaned. "First it's Sooty now it's Cilla Black..."

"Wrong again, ol' green scales!" Hadlee sniggered.

And they all sang rousing choruses of *It's A Long Way To Tipp-a-Dragon* and *Okie Cokie, Knees Bend Baa, Baaa, Baaa.*

Fêted with Praise

Stop press news: Embers has won the Tour de France. You hadn't heard? Well, the answer to that is simple. When his Dragonship completed his entry form for the race, in error he filled in a lottery ticket... simple mistake, could happen to anyone... and he put a cross in the box for 'no publicity'. Consequently his triumph remains a secret between you and me.

Saturday: the village fête. After a quiet word in the committee's ear, Embers, our local hero, is invited to open the proceedings. Talk about fame going to a dragon's head. The conceited what-not is strutting around, practising his waving, looking for his ceremonial scissors, composing his speech, and asking at every given moment if Sue Lawley has telephoned about his 'Desert Island Discs' yet. (*Puff the Magic Dragon*, *Cwym Rhondda*, *Smoke Gets in your Eyes* and *Dragons of Harlech* – his luxury is a photograph of himself with the Queen Mother!)

Traditionally the fête starts off with a parade from Bowood's 'Golden Gate' to the school where this afternoon's attractions will commence at two. The Chippenham Sea Scouts Band leads the way with a stirring rendition of *Life on the Ocean Wave*. There is a children's fancy dress parade, Cubs and Brownies and everyone has a balloon and falls over their feet trying to keep in time with the music. Embers, wearing his winner's medal, pedals furiously to keep up with them, stopping to sign autographs for the local postmaster and his family along the way (huh!).

2 p.m. Arrive at school, Embers loses scissors, gets tied up in his ceremonial ribbon, loses his script and does an impromptu tap dance to cover his confusion. He is a sensation!

He allows me to accompany him round the stalls and to take photographs of him with the village dignitaries. The vicar is 'enchanted' to meet him (isn't everyone?), Akala wants him to join cubs (he'll never cope with the woggle), and the Sea Scouts want him as a mascot (snigger). Suddenly, out from the marquee leaps Firefighter Newman, lecturer in fire prevention, who asks Mr Dragon to leave immediately as he is causing a conflagration hazard near the Scouts' barbecue. Rendered speechless, we pedal home.

Now, fête or no fête, the most exciting thing to hit Studley every year is the village pig roast. Luckily it doesn't require 'opening'. There is always a grand raffle and everyone is generous at parting with the pennies and donating prizes.

Monday: the postman arrives with a letter for Embers from the Royal Ballet (news travels fast). An irregular-shaped package is not addressed to 'yours sheepishly', and I ignore it. Suddenly, without warning, not a 'by your leave' to be heard, out from the parcel jumps this white whirlwind of a thing apparently under the name of 'Russ' (Conway perhaps?). He announces that HE is a raffle prize... whatever next...

It chattered away, nineteen to the dozen, organising this, rearranging that, and made me sigh a long nostalgic sigh for my dear old pal Embers who's spending the day on a 'round Wales' lap of honour. Almost a relief to go off to school early for a quick practice of *Joseph*. The Misses Parker and Kimber who remember the Young Master as an even younger master with white knobbly knees who couldn't tie his shoelaces come in to listen.

The headmaster puts his head round the door, "Sounds like Blackpool Tower in here," he quips and disappears before I can ask him the Tower Ballroom's phone number.

Back home Russ is tinkering with the keyboard. We seem to be getting a mite too fond of him, methinks... at least he doesn't wave, he claps and as he passes a faint whiff of fish accompanies him.

The dress rehearsal: the orchestra sounds as if someone's mixed up the music, Joseph has to step over the flautists to reach the stage, and a palm tree finds it all too much and fells itself. The choir forget to sing and stand up and sit down in all the wrong places, Mr Birch collapses Pharaoh's palace (poor, poor Pharaoh, what'cha gonna do?) and we sigh with relief as the Young Master hits the final notes of *Any Dream Will Do* in approximately the right order.

Tuesday: The Performance. With the old adage 'bad dress rehearsal, good performance' being muttered at every turn, every toe and finger crossed and a knot tied in Embers' tail for luck, we take our seats. Bounce opens the popcorn, Moley has his tape-recorder.

"Someone is playing *Match of the Day* on the organ," whispers Hayzee, "I wonder who...?" as the last of the proud parents arrive. Russ opens a tin of sardines, Mrs Wackett dims the lights and we're off...

The overture, although a little long for the average opera-loving sheep, sounds good, and everyone remembers their words in the prologue. Joseph appears on cue wearing THE coat which "certainly took the biscuit, and was the smoothest in the district, he was handsome, he was smart, he was a walking..." copy of his mother's curtains and the Young Master's fingers were flashing over the keys as we went through red and yellow and green and azure and ochre and peach and olive and violet and orange and blue. (Memo: perhaps Mrs Wackett would like me to write a little something for next year's extravaganza.)

Mr Birch gets Mrs Birch to help him. Okay the palm tree's still not too happy and 'Benjamin' is spotted wearing his digital Egyptian watch but everything else goes like clockwork. Myself, perhaps I'm biased, but I thought the cardboard cut-out sheep on the hill were the stars of the show – and there wasn't a dragon in sight, except for the one snoring next to me... anyone spare an old Egyptian sock?

Australians, Royalty and Revelry

It has been decided by 'The Committee' that the annual Village Barbecue should be coupled with celebrations for the birthday of – that local celebrity – Embers the Dragon. The announcement was in the *Gazette and Herald*... did you miss it?

Much hammering of posts and tent pegs heralds the start of Studley's most entertaining weekend of the year. Since it's usually the only village event this fact cannot be disputed.

The Patch, usually desolate apart from the Young Master's goal net, a dilapidated old tractor (related to Terrence that cheeky pal of Thomas the Tank Engine) and the odd dog out on exercise, is a positive hive of activity. Marquees are raised around the perimeter and tables and chairs set out. Looking across the dip (shudder) towards Bremhill, straw bales, flags and stakes are delivered in readiness for the 'clay pigeon shoot'.

Signs are erected: 'Ice Cream', 'Car Park', 'Penalty Shoot-out' and 'Skittles'.

The Andrews Sisters are singing *Don't Sit Under the Apple Tree* whilst polishing Embers' bike which will be on a podium in the main tent. He says he has 'video footage of his triumph' but... it has been mislaid. Bunting and balloons are hung on the marquees and the Red Flash is practising his speech whilst rehearsing the (still polishing) Andrews Sisters in their rendering of *Happy Birthday dear Dragon*. He has asked the Queen Mother to open the festivities but I fear a 'previous engagement' and divert him to the barbecue.

Embers sneezes, nearly igniting more than the barbecue. Firefighter Newman has reason to be concerned, Ol' Green Scales claims to have hay fever. Someone has cut the grass and the cuttings are blowing everywhere, especially into the clean glasses just delivered with a firkin or three of 'Ferrets Favourite', a barrel of lager and copious amounts of wine.

Saturday morning: the day dawns, as they say, bright and clear. Embers is respectfully requested (sigh) to light the barbecue. During this ceremony the jolly postman arrives, Embers investigates his bike, and does a couple of laps of The Patch to practise his waving (it's best to humour him). I glance at the letters: one with rather a grand seal (not Russ) for his Dragonship. Two for me, one with an Australian stamp. (NB, why do Australian stamps always feature kookaburras and surfboarders? Why not a surfboarding kookaburra and be done with it?) And a postcard for Russ (didn't know raffle prizes received postcards).

Russ, that other sort of seal, regiments the raffle prizes: flowers, whisky, wine, chocolates, a framed (and signed) photograph of Embers the Dragon. Russ arranged himself next to a brace of trout – thinking of my Australian letter I hoped a passing Antipodean might win him and transport him and his opera back to the outback... fingers (and Dragon's tail's knotted) crossed.

I take five minutes to read my letter: it's from a Jason Donovan, a much accoladed actor from Adelaide and a singer as well. It seems Mr Lloyd Webber, busy with the tunes for *Malteser Merino* has mentioned the musical to Mr Donovan. Mr Donovan is keen to play the romantic lead 'Hadlee Sheep' and would be pleased to meet with me to discuss terms. Mint sauce!! Tal Bonc the singing greengrocer... perhaps.

My other letter is from Cameron Macintosh who is very keen to be involved with my musical. He suggests the London Palladium... I'll think about that.

2 p.m. Changed into our smartest clothes (myself, I favoured a liberty print bow tie), we return to The Patch for 'The Shoot'. Now, it's one thing nabbing a clay pigeon but quite another knowing the best way to barbecue one. Even with copious amounts of ketchup they proved tough and I decided to wait for a sizzled sausage later.

Russ, his opera complete (sigh) says he has invited Dame Joan Sutherland along for a preview of his work which he will perform at sunset – just before he's 'raffled'. The postcard is from her, she will arrive at five after a day with friends in Berkshire. Russ announces, just for Dame Joan, he will then sing, as an encore, *My Way* (his way, indeed!) and *Climb Every Mountain* in honour of Embers' achievement in the Tour de France.

4 p.m. The Grand Opening Ceremony. The revellers gather. The Andrews Sisters sing *Happy Birthday* and the vicar presents Embers with the villagers' birthday gift to him: wrapped in scarlet and gold striped paper and tied with a scarlet ribbon, it is a portrait of the Red Flash holding his Tour de France Trophy aloft. (NB, why is the trophy inscribed 'Wimbledon and District Chambers of Commerce, William Goater Challenge Cup' – was the aforementioned Mr Goater a famous bicyclist or was he, as I suspect, an estate agent.)

The Andrews Sisters then hum *Cwym Rhondda* as the Red Flash gives his inevitable and endless speech of thanks...

The bar is open, the Ferrets Favourite is sampled and ice creams are licked. The Young Master takes on all comers in his 'penalty shoot-out': there are chocolate footballs to be won! A young German lad called 'Jurgan' seems to be doing well.

Mrs Klinsman consults Gypsy Rose Madder (those little red ears are strikingly familiar) and crosses her palm with silver. "I see the colours blue and red, someone called Eric, a football team, a crown, the initials B and M and VP and flowers...

Mrs Klinsman goes on to win a bottle of best British Sherry for the flower arranging competition.

"I could have won that," sniffed Embers, "I think I'll borrow a book from the library and have a go next year."

And a French poodle called 'Eric' wins the dog agility competition.

"I could have done that too," said Embers.

"You're not a dog," I pointed out.

"Woof woof," he replied. "I'm a red setter!"

Everything was going well, a flotilla of balloons drift over, a bearded man in a Fair Isle jumper leans out and waves. The village is having fun but where is the cabaret? The 'Bumpkin Boffins' are late!

We go into a huddle: we could stand in... but what to call ourselves? 'Hadlee and the Golden Fleeces', 'The Flickering Embers'? We already knew a close harmony on my favourite song, *Baah, Baaah, Baah, Baaah Baa-bra Anne* and we could improvise in the best jazz traditions... or perform our Baah-Baah Shop Quartet routine: Embers was already wearing his waistcoat and Hayzee and Bounce had their straw hats.

Too late, the 'Boffins' arrived and soon we were tapping our toes. Embers, with his terpsichorean tendencies, capered away to all the sixties hits and more. He 'Hippy, Hippy Shook', he rocked, he rolled, he jived, he jitterbugged.

7 p.m. The raffle. The first ticket is drawn by the vicar. Ticket no. 13 – the Young Master – and he takes his pick of the prizes... I suppose we'll get accustomed to opera and the bouquet of sardines... Second ticket: Dame Joan wins an inflatable kangaroo. Third ticket: the Vicar himself – *Mr Dragon's Book of Bicycle Maintenance*.

"Pity he didn't win the kangaroo," whispers Ernie. "Very handy for hopping to the post office to cash a postal order."

Dancing till dusk: on with the fairy lights and Embers Travolta (whose dancing has previously been reported to the Friends of the Royal Ballet) is the sensation of the evening. Ernie gives us his *Birdie Song*, thank you, Ernie, and Edward recites his ghostly monologue 'Southampton Sid'.

Sitting around the remains of the fire, Embers wonders what happened to the Queen Mother. Affairs of state, tea with our other absentee, Dame Joan, or the last race at Ascot have detained her, he supposes.

I remember his letter, which is propped up against his trophy in the marquee. It's from an 'Elizabeth Windsor' entreating him to let her audition for the part of Embers the Dragon in the stage musical *Malteser Merino* (foolishly I appointed him producer). She sends a photograph.

"That horse looks just like me," chips in Bounce, "taken at some parade or other..."

What shall the Dragon do? He's already promised the part to Bonnie Langford.

The Four Fanatics!

Russ and Moley are plotting something! They've been upstairs for hours 'tweaking' the cat's whiskers (cat far from happy) and muttering 'coley'.

At first I thought this was a reference to Moley's old friend from the Kensington boutique where they both spent their early days. They often exchange postcards – a tradition started by Moley the day he had his adventure on the London Underground and ended up bumping into the Red Menace at Paddington station and coming to live with us.

Coley dreamt of a career in the theatre and to star every Christmas in *Wind in the Willows*, they listened every evening to Radio Four and Coley and Moley still meet every summer for a holiday under a garden shed in Weymouth. They eat enormous helpings of Coq-au-ver and exchange gossip and news of their favourite programmes on the radio.

The two moles have a vast circle of friends in Savernake Forest. This ramshackle crew have never featured on *Down Your Way* and would only be mentioned on *Gardener's Question Time* if they came up for air in the middle of an immaculate lawn. At 'Mole End' they spend their days annoying hoity-toity Marlborough ladies

with gardening gloves, secateurs and trugs full of roses. They would never send a card – even on the occasion of a birthday.

Moley loves his radio, especially *The Archers* (he's a founder member of the Eddie Grundy Fan Club and has the cowboy hat to prove it!) and his most treasured possessions are his scrapbook of *Radio Times* cuttings and his autographed photograph of Irene Thomas.

He enjoys *The Farming Programme* (unless eradicating moles is on the agenda) and has written a note to Ned Sherrin about his ideas for *Start The Week* and to *Sport on 4* about his plans for under soil heating (it involves much tunnelling) at Twickenham. Back to 'coley'. It's all sounding a bit fishy to a sheep. The other day it was *Gardener's Question Time* and a septuagenarian cat lover was heard to say that she fed her cat on fish and her clematis on the milk in which it was cooked. This procedure she had followed (with various cats and the same clematis) for forty years. The clematis had died. What should she do?

Russ was laughing at this so much that his piano lid dropped on his flipper which, in turn, made Moley laugh. They both collapsed in gales of howling laughter... and missed the answer. They are tuning in again to catch the repeat of *The Mystery of the Coley, the Cat and the Clematis*!

Hold Very Tight, Please!

Monday: Embers still searching the pages of *Exchange & Mart* for a second hand Jumbo 'one careful owner, low mileage' etc., etc. Decides that a bit of adventure is the order of the day...

We overhear that a day trip to London is planned. I take my notepad to record our trip.

Sneaking into a carrier bag, Embers is almost completely camouflaged by a scarlet pac-a-mac and I disguise myself inside a large packet of tissues... I'll be well equipped if I catch a cold!

Up the A4, past the white horse etched in the hillside and on to Marlborough, passing a very early morning jogger in lime green lycra, the radio played *Baah Baah Baah Baaah Baa-bra Anne*, The Bear at Hungerford and at The Tally Ho, *Tally Ho*! Half way up the M4 we took a decko... weather fine... traffic light... we'd soon be there... wonder if they'll stop at the new service station... isn't that junction 12?

Docklands, and we get our bearings. The old Surrey Docks look nothing like they did in their heyday, all that remains is a memory in a black and white photograph. Windsurfers sail and yachts and dinghies bob in the water replacing the great cargo ships and seafaring traditions for which the area was once renowned.

Tobacco and Empire Wharves, Greenland Dock, Ropemakers Fields, Hornblower Way, Norway Gate, Finland Street, Quebec Way, modern recollections of days gone... and the 'Wibbly Wobbly'?... a non ocean-going vessel of a wine bar!

A few early commuters, a lone fisherman and a cormorant, both seeking the same catch, are the only evidence of activity at this early hour. A lone light glints from an office window. A burglar alarm sounds without warning. The local duck population ignores it – they've heard it all before. The air traffic light atop the Canary Wharf Tower winks knowingly in the background.

Soon, we find ourselves on a bus (not a red one, to Embers' disgust), London Transport, diesel engined, 97 horsepower, omni variety of same.

I decide, if a career in journalism is for Hadlee, that an inconsequential bus journey will make a challenging report... Embers? He's busy trying to persuade the driver to let him have a turn at the wheel.

We board the romantically dubbed 'P11' destination: Waterloo. 'Welcome to Surrey Quays' the hoarding enthuses. With its modern shopping mall and executive housing it contrasts vividly with the tatty tenements and short-lease shops surrounding it.

Our journey will take us though residential streets lined with dolls' house like dwellings, brick pavements with decorative mock Victorian railings (and matching bus stops) guarding ornamental shrubs and regimented trees set out just as the architect planned it!

The City Farm, Fisher Athletic Football Ground, the huge gasometer of the South Eastern Gas Board, meeting the needs of the metropolis. 'Lavender Dock' conjured up more thoughts of time long past and, would you 'Adam and Eve' it, a rather seedy pub stands on the corner by Rotherhithe Station as we leave behind the smart yuppie houses and begin our run down Jamaica Road. I use my mobile phone to arrange a meeting with my editor.

The bus is full. The traffic queue is already building up for the tunnel in the other direction, north to Shadwell and Limehouse.

Early morning, chattering children en route for school fill the top deck. Their peers peer over their newspapers or tap a foot to silent music on their Walkman and cackling charladies, their day's work done, discuss their cronies as street signs and landmarks flash past. It seems to be a popular haunt for dentists. Surgeries seem to be on every corner, next to the takeaway and the sweet shop... perhaps the jolting buses are loosening the passengers' teeth?

Southwark Park on our left, early morning joggers and dog walkers dodge and weave. The 'Trusty Pet Shop', the 'Fisherman's Friend', a launderette, chemist and the 'Gregorian' public house, are still shuttered against nocturnal visitors.

The bus lurches and swings down Druid Street, underneath the arches, voluminous rubbish sacks are stacked and ready to be gobbled up by the next dust-cart. Crucifix Lane and buddleia abounds in the nooks and crannies of time-worn brickwork. A splash of colour in a grey landscape.

We turn 'one way' under the railway, towards London Bridge station. A train sparkling in the sunshine is reflected in the huge first floor windows of the newly refurbished Hays Depository. 'My Teashop' is guarded by a huge German Shepherd (perhaps he's strayed from the 'London Dungeon' next door?). Was he really good for business? Sandwich bars jostle for the attention of the day's workforce seeking breakfast or an early lunch.

A glimpse of Southwark Cathedral, Blackfriars Bridge Road and the lights are on red to allow a fleet of bicycling 'executives', pin-striped suits, briefcases neatly furled umbrella and cycle clips, to pedal on to the office. Towards Waterloo another red light. We pull up by 'Kirkaldy's Testing Works' with a curious motto carved in stone over the door: 'Facts not Opinions'.

Waterloo: all change for the train.

The Dragon Now Standing on Platform 18...

Waterloo: "Perhaps next time we'll hijack a Eurostar," whispers Embers as we climb the steps of the station entrance.

This grand portico is a tribute to the age of steam, we could easily be entering a grand Edwardian hotel or theatre... in those days they did things properly.

Our intrepid dragon scampers off to WH Smith for postcards. He's recently discovered that Welsh stamps bear the added symbol of a Welsh dragon and can only imagine that Elizabeth (Regina not Green) has decided that HE is a better lick than her own gracious majesty's profile, and she is stepping down from the role.

He returns, hotfoot, with breakfast and a slim volume of John Betjeman for yours sheepishly. We duck quickly back into the carrier bag and because of this I cannot be quite certain how at 9.31 we were munching a cheeseburger by the 'Cheap Day Return' window and at 9.32 we were gambolling along platform 18 in pursuit of the Richmond train... just as the guard was blowing his trusty whistle. (Memo: whatever happened to the Fat Controller and that cheeky little blue engine of his?)

"Where's the engine?" asks Embers. "There must be a proper engine, even the Island of Sodor has proper engines."

"It's electric," I explain.

With a huff and a puff he scrambles up into the luggage rack and sulks.

"I was expecting the Bournemouth Belle, something like old 35022," (some of his best friends are engines) "not a jumped up electric thing; I want something Merchant Navy class, Lord Nelson or that fiery old 'East Asiatic Company'... those were the days. Did you know, by the way," (he puffed out his chest) "that there was a train called *The Red Dragon*? Pride of the Paddington line... A35... Great Western trains don't look like that any more. Where's the steam, where's the smokebox? Where's the glamour? *Princess Margaret Rose* or the *Duchess of Montrose*. *Evening Star*, where's the romance? Did you ever hear of *Brief Encounter on the Richmond Line*? Where's the Pullman, Doris and Dora and Dulcie and the mystique, and how do I thank the driver?"

Mystique, I must admit, did not abound, overland trains are not what they were. South London holds many attractions but most of them aren't visible from any train bound (all stations) for Strawberry Hill.

Battersea Power Station, an empty shell of its former self, is advertising 'Bungee Jumping': 9.35 on a Wednesday morning – no customers. Through Queenstown Road, we crept on towards darkest Clapham, crawled by the 'train-wash' (shudder) and up to the Junction. Will we arrive on time At this rate, never! Even the doors sigh as they close.

As we pull away from Clapham, the busiest railway junction in the country, we gather speed. The wonders of Wandsworth Town, clickety-click, clickety-click, pulsating Putney, clickety-click, clickety-click, Barnes, Barnes, barnstorming through Barnes.

Level crossing gates in our favour at Mortlake, pretty terraced houses, window boxes, ornamental shutters and garden swings. Washing blowing like semaphore signals in the breeze. Allotted allotments growing runner beans and flowers... and very soon after Richmond was reached.

Richmond station: we walk through the town, the sun's shining and the sheep may safely graze down by the river bank. What tales it could tell! (Memo: one can only safely graze after one has learnt to avoid on-coming bicycles.)

We dip our toes in the water, write a postcard to Ernie (and stand on each other's shoulders to reach the pillar-box) and follow the towpath to Kingston-on-Thames.

The river bus hoots, and the passengers wave. In his excitement Embers waves back and takes a bow... and falls in the river. A Canada Goose (always so helpful Canadians) fishes him out and we hang him, by his tail, on the washing line of a passing narrow boat to dry out. He steams, gently. I take the tiller for a while, the Canada Goose takes a photograph (why do Canadians always photograph things?) and shows me snapshots of his numerous relations back home (yawn). They are all wearing 'Raptors' baseball caps, carrying ice hockey sticks and don't look as though they have even a slim chance of 'getting their man'.

A passing convoy of mallards think this is all very amusing (they've obviously seen the album), till Embers, still topsy turvey on his line, mutters 'orange sauce' at them and they scuttle off to the far bank and the safety of the boathouse.

Finally, we reach Kingston, we wave goodbye to our friends on the narrow boat, a Mr Toad and his friend Ratty... their horse 'Albert', a fine dappled grey (looked a bit like our Dessie – if the silver framed photograph was a true likeness) wasn't with them today as he'd nipped off to take part in the 2.30 at Kempton Park. We wished them luck and promised to pop in the betting shop and put a half crown on Albert for the St Ledger.

Via the sports shop for a pair of 'Spurs' socks for the Young Master's birthday to 'John Lewis' the department store, for the meeting with my editor.

"Nice here," says Embers. "Sort of place Edward would like, very classy, very Southampton – let's buy him a present! Let's buy everyone a present."

Generous to a fault, he chooses a large painting of an orchard for Hayzee, a lamp in the shape of the Statue of Liberty for Ernie, a large wicker picnic hamper for Bounce, a handmade patchwork quilt for Coley and for Runcie: "After shave?... Aqua de what??... very useful gift," snorts Embers nearly setting light to a 'novelty pipe-smokers kit' nearby.

Miss Tarragon, for that's my editor, wishes to discuss my new book *Dragon Rampant*, a biography of a 'famous aviator' and *Malteser Merino*: 'The Book of the Millenium' (my suggestion). She mentions termination clauses', 'cover prices', 'marketing plans', 'targets'. That sort of thing.

The Red Menace wanders off and finds himself in the ladies' lingerie department. He is returned by the security guard, carrying his purchases, and wearing a very fetching camisole in 'shell pink'.

"Not my fault," he argued, turning even more scarlet than usual (and clashing appallingly with his new underwear). "I thought it said 'linger here' and as I was bored it seemed just the place to go."

I thanked the security man, gave him my autograph on a £5 note and returned to Miss Tarragon who was busy totting up a column of 'forward sales'.

"We can just afford a cup of tea," she announced, gleefully.

"Can I have one?" asked Embers (with his camisole safely in a carrier bag – what would he do with it? Surely it's not for Edward?

"Not this week," replied Miss Tarragon with a sideways glance at the menu and price-list.

Over tea and a lightly buttered scone (Embers chooses the tea cake and, for economy, toasts it himself), we talk about personal appearances, book signings. Green scales were now quivering to the tune of gentle snoring, the Young Master's new socks were proving useful, already.

Miss Tarragon decides, then and there, to take a photograph of me for the dust jacket of my tome. Lights, action!

"You can't do that here... it's against company policy," says our hitherto polite waitress.

It will be a different story when I return to sign copies of my number one best-seller!

Bramble Gets the Bird

Tuesday: I was sitting at the kitchen table – as most authors do – chewing the end of my pencil and pondering on my next chapter or six, when... from down the garden came a strange noise.

Not Embers tuning his bike or the Andrews Sisters' three-part harmony (similar). Not a 'woof woof I'm barking because I like annoying the neighbours' sort of noise, not distant lawnmower doing a bowling green finish to a neighbouring lawn or the Air Force, up above, on manoeuvres, but a scuffly, squeaky, squawly sort of noise...

In a trice there appeared in the kitchen a chicken. Not any old broiler, you understand, but one of the next door neighbours' 'Silkys': a small, elegant white glamorous thing given to posing in (or out of) its run, so that one might fully admire its beauty.

This bird was closely followed, rather too closely for comfort, by Bramble – the terrier-ist...

Now, some of my best friends are chickens (and some of the best actors on Sesame Street – sorry, Ernie), and I felt I ought to be refereeing this state of affairs. This unscheduled cabaret was the last thing I needed! Feathers were flying all over my new laptop computer. Perhaps it would just fly out again? Is life that simple?

By this time Tealeaf, the spaniel, had cottoned on to the fact that a game was on, and the three of them did a circuit of the kitchen before leaving the way they'd arrived... now closely followed by the lady of the house (who'd been lightly chopping a few mushrooms) waving a tea towel!

Have you ever counted the number of feathers a chicken can lose whilst circuiting a kitchen? Plenty, and they flutter to the oddest places – probably even a David Shilling hat if there's a garden party up the Mall. (Come to think of it, some Ascot milliners, out to be noticed, would dump a whole chicken on a hat without batting an eyelid.) Well, it all brightens a dull day.

It's 'Bob A Job' week and, of course, the Young Master is out there, scarf and woggle at its usual rakish angle, doing his bit. I ought, by word of explanation, to mention that a 'bob' is an old fashioned nickname for an equally old fashioned shilling now worth the sum total of an amazing five pence and not recommended as payment to a Boy Scout unless you require a brick through your window the following day.

I digress. Old dib, dib, dib, has been round all the neighbours and relieved them of their milk money for hanging out the washing and sweeping a path. He's cleaned two cars and 'minded' a goat. Not sure how much the goat minded but they both survived the experience.

Don't Let the Cat out of the Bag

The Young Master and his parents are planning a trip to a 'Country Show'. Now, that sort of thing is not my idea of entertainment: all that livestock! Ferrets and polecats... and... sheepdog trials... the ultimate horror story.

And it's raining! Bet they're having puddles of fun.

We are cosy, at home, catching up on all those little jobs we meant to do and didn't. Embers is replying to his fan mail (yawn) and is busy signing photographs in his best Dragon Script.

I have taken the opportunity to type up a few pages of the script of *Malteser Merino* on the Young Master's mum's word processor. (I'm sure she doesn't mind, it must be exciting having a famous writer in the house.)

Hayzee, Bounce, Moley and Edward are playing Trivial Pursuits. Hayzee is in the final furlong, he's landed on all the 'nature' squares and seems to have invented his own section on the 'Geography of the New Forest'. Would you know where the Knightwood Oak or Tyrrells Ford were?

Well, Moley reckons he once tunnelled under the Knightwood Oak whilst on holiday at Mark Ash Wood and Edward is positive that Tyrrells Ford is near Tyrell and Green, the Southampton emporium where all the best bears have afternoon tea (yawn). Wrong Edward – there is a spare, damp 'r' in the ford and whoever heard of a stream running through a shop? "Well in Southampton, us bears!..." Old sock anyone??

Ernie (baseball hat on back to front as usual) is practising with his clapperboard. "Scene 1 Take 99 – Embers the Dragon, waving to camera" ... Clap... "Ouch!", he's caught his nose for the ninety-ninth time.

I'm re-writing the scene where I win the bear 'Aloysius' at the Goatacre Fête (in case you're wondering, I keep him on a very high shelf next to a packet of Persil) and checking Mr Lloyd Webber's latest ideas for the music for the Maltese Bicycling Song (to a cha-cha rhythm – he hasn't got to ride the bike!), before asking Russ to play it.

I turn to give the music to Russ, who puts down a half-empty tin of mackerel (his third) and starts to play the keyboard. Meanwhile, back at the other keyboard Kiwi, the Young Master's cat, has curled up for afternoon nap.

This is the very same furry feline who can eat its way through half a tin of the best Kitty bits at one sitting and then go out and dine on a shrew; the very same cat that trips the light fantastic, with a routine that Torvill and Dean would envy, on the conservatory roof: the very black beast that comes in around three in the morning, soaking wet, and curls up on 'our' bed. In need of a little extra beauty sleep, the keyboard, it seems, is just the place.

What now, I must finish my edit before teatime? I push, I shove, I cajole and all I hear is a sleepy 'purr'.

"Should have stuck to the spiral notepad," mutters Embers, "this is much to technical for a sheep." Mint sauce!

The Red Menace gives a helpful shove with Ernie's clapperboard, zilch, and then he remembers Russ's mackerel. We wave it under the cat's nose – "Action, lights, camera", he shouts. "Take one tin of mackerel," (now he thinks he's Delia Smith) – and in a flash Kiwi is off in pursuit of the enticingly fishy aroma.

Horror upon horrors! All was not well, everything was coming out on 34-line pages. This, I argued with the machine, just would not do. There should be 54 lines to the page and it's 54 I want, 52... maybe... 56 would be acceptable but not 34: 'people' will notice!

Out came the manual, and I seemed to have cracked it – well, we arrived at 37 by jamming Embers' tail in the printer and using headers and footers to advantage and with me keeping one elbow on the page break control button. I was stuck, so was the dragon. A dark shape loomed over us. Kiwi, with a satisfied 'miaow' returned, turned round three times on Embers' head to get comfortable and, in the twitch of a whisker, was fast asleep. Another fine mess... footsteps on the stairs... and a strange 'squeak'.

"Sooty, that's all we need," mumbled Embers from under Kiwi's head. The Young Master had returned with a strange grey individual with a bushy tail, white paws and an Arsenal football shirt. "Squeak, squeak," it repeated. (Typical Arsenal fan, limited vocabulary.) "Poor Embers," sympathised the Young Master and cautiously pulled him out from under the comatosed quadruped and hugged him. Green scales fell like rain and the Young Master took him downstairs to watch *Noel's House Party* (as a treat?) after his hideous ordeal.

"Squeak, would you Adam and Eve it, a stuck sheep," said the squeaky person. "I'm the 'Wright' person to help, here. Paul Merson wouldn't leave a sheep in a shambles, neither will I..." And, with a distinct lack of dignity, he pulled me out... that was a narrow squeak!

Formally introduced a few minutes later, my liberator told me his name was 'Squirry' and that he had been chosen, from a stall of woodland folk puppets, by the Young Master as a new companion for us. Another Trivial Pursuits fan, he was invited to join the game.

From where did the Mayflower set sail in 1620 and the Titanic in 1912? Quick as a flash, "Southampton," answers our new chum.

"I knew that," grumbled Edward. Nature: to what family do gophers and marmots belong? "Sciuridae Squirrels!!" squeaks Squirry. I like this game!"

But soft, what light from yonder window breaks, 'tis the Young Master's mum investigating her computer. With a rattle of the piggy bank (it's 50p a minute) the helpline was dialled...

"Utterly impossible," said the young lady on the other end of the phone. And she went through her 'button pressing by telephone' formula to see what misfortune had befallen her state-of-the-art machine. "It's still impossible,' she said, as after what seemed like half an hour (you add it up – I daren't) she put it right. You'd need at least three hands to have done that... or four paws, a dragon's tail and a tired cat, perhaps?

'Our' room is to be redecorated. At present it is a country cottage collection of pine and patchwork set against a symphony of flowers. It's not been changed since I was invited to stay, although the cot has been replaced by a bed and soon we will have a cabin bed (much recommended if you sleep with a dragon – you can keep him in the drawer underneath). The cabin bed will

come flat-packed, that should be fun. It will have a piece missing or the instructions will be in Japanese... I think I'll join Kiwi on the keyboard, it's beginning to sound quite cosy.

Embers has a notion for something loud and red with regency stripes and his portrait over the fireplace. Moley would like sponged 'warm earth', Bounce has a yen for an equestrian theme and Hayzee would like a New Forest mural (à la Hilda Ogden, complete with flying ducks?). Myself? Just call me an old fashioned sort of sheep – I'd stick with the flower power... perhaps the Young Master should choose, it's his name on the door. Whatever happens, it's bound to be chaos, and that Dragon will probably put his foot in the paste bucket or get stuck behind the paper.

Now, the Young Master informs me. "I'm not a flower sort of boy" and he has a fancy for stencils or preferably a Tottenham Hotspurs motif! With all his posters and paraphernalia I can't really see the need for wallpaper... but, boys will be boys and we've narrowed it down to four including the super Spurs job.

"Spurs," squeaks Squirry. "Spurs? I can't have cockerels all over the walls, I'll have nightmares. It's bad enough living under a 'Teddy' Sherringham poster."

("Not another bear," groans Embers from under the cat who's taken quite a fancy to him as a pillow.)

The Trivial Pursuits board is still out. Television: what type of puppet did Harry Corbett groom for stardom? Business: what name is given to a speculator on the stock exchange?

"I can't bear it any longer," says Embers as he slithers out from under the cat and finds he's moved two places on the Trivial Pursuit board without even shaking the dice!

And if he can answer what is the national Flower of Wales? Wait, wait, he can: daffodil! He's won, game set and match to Mr Dragon. His prize? An all expenses paid trip to see Sooty in pantomime (snigger).

Malteser Merino

Cast in order of appearance

WALES:

Betws-y-Coed (Embers' Mother)	*Elizabeth Bowes Lyon*
Embers the Dragon	*Himself*
Ffestinigog Dragon (his brother)	*Tom Jones*
Blaenau Cader Idris (Tiger) his sister	*Shirley Bassey*
Embers the Dragon (equestrian sequence)	*Elizabeth Windsor*

NEW ZEALAND:

Hadlee the Sheep (as a lamb)	*Sir Cliff Richard*
Sir Edmund Hillary Sheep (a famous explorer)	*Himself*
Hadlee the Sheep	*Himself*
Grandbaa-baa Sheep	*Dame Peggy Ashcroft*
Mrs Sheep (Hadlee's Mother)	*Dame Judi Dench*

WILTSHIRE/LONDON:

Sooty's Gang	*Paddington Bear*
	Winnie the Pooh
	Rupert Bear
	Super Ted

A Knight in Shining Armour	*Alec Stewart*
Thursday Knight	*Sir Richard Hadlee*
Nightclub singer	*Dame Kiri Te Kanawa*

The Andrews Sisters	*Badminton Bounce*
	Hayzee the Horse
	Moley the Mole

King Edward VII	*Edward Bear*
A dark, mysterious stranger	*G.W. Gilbert*
His henchman	*Bonnie Langford*
Tal Bonc – the singing greengrocer	*Michael Ball*

Squiggles the Bear by kind permission of Miss Tarragon
Hadlee the Sheep's relations on loan from *The Archers*

Original music by Russ the Seal.
Theme music *Malteser Merino* performed by
Milly Molly Manley and the Milestones.
Dance routines by Dame Heidi Hunt
under the direction of Embers the Dragon.

Mr Hadlee Sheep and G.W. Gilbert's wardrobe by
Gieves & Peake of Bognor Regis.
Wardrobe mistress Maureen Janes.
Washing powder by Persil.
Coathangers by 'Hipi Hangers'.
Bicycle loaned by the Vicar.

for FLEECE FILMS

Executive Producer	Embers the Dragon
Screenplay	Hadlee Sheep
Lighting and Special Effects	Squirry's Squad
Clapperboard, Continuity and Megaphone	Ernie
Mobile Catering	Runcie's Lunchie Munchies
Floral arrangements	Embers' Elite Embellishments

Colour by Felt Tip

Scene 1. The foot of Mount Snowdon.
Snow, smoke curling from a cosy collage, from inside: singing *Cwym Rhondda.*
Betws-y-Coed appears with her family carrying a baby dragon.

Scene 2. New Zealand.
A famous explorer sits with his great nephew recalling his mountaineering exploits in the Himalayas and Snowdonia.
Climb Every Mountain – Dame Kiri Te Kanawa.

Scene 3. New Zealand. Two years later.
Hadlee the Sheep leaves for England.
Medley: *Now is the Hour/We'll keep a Welcome in the Hillside* (arr. R.S.).
Dame Kiri Te Kanawa/Embers the Dragon.

Scene 4. Harvey Nichols' toy department.
Hobby Horse Derby *Ascot Gavotte.*
Two Little Boys – duet – Badminton Bounce, Hayzee the Horse.
Teddy Bear's Picnic – Sooty's Gang – recorder solo, the Young Master

Scene 5. Knight-Time... a fantasy.
Original lyrics: Sir Tim Rice, music R.S.

Scene 6. Deepest Wiltshire.
Cabin Bed Capers – the Andrews Sisters with H.S.

Scene 7. Mount Snowdon.
The Glove Puppet Emporium with E.D. NB, cancel Sooty.

Scene 8. The Red Dragon... a celebration of the age of steam.
E.D., *Men of Harlech, Theme from Murder on the Orient Express, Coronation Scot, In Town Tonight.*
Medley arr. Russ the Seal.

Scene 9. London.
London Cries medley (by R.S. in collaboration with Sir Andrew Lloyd Webber) with Buckingham Palace backdrop.(Guest appearance King Edward VII.)
Bicycle acrobatics: with Q.M. Equine Extravaganza – Horsing Around with Badminton Bounce, Hayzee the Horse and 'B' Platoon Household Cavalry.

Scene 10. Wembley on the P11 bus.
Football Fantasia. Guest Conductor: Steve Allman, *You'll never Walk Alone* F.C. Chippenham.
Solo: the Young Master.

Scene 11. Wiltshire: Symphony on a Suitcase.
Summer Holiday – Sir Cliff Richard and Ensemble.

Scene 12. London Airport: 'Abracadabra' magical moments.
Disappearing passport routine song and dance.
Mr Gollivator by G. W. Gilbert.
Boogie Woogie Baggage Boys of Terminal Three.
The Andrews Sisters.

Scene 13. Malta.
Stunt flying by Squiggles the Bear – wing walking by Sooty.

Grand finale.
Featuring Embers the Dragon, Hadlee Sheep and the whole company.

NB, FILE UNDER 'C' FOR CAT – TOP SECRET

Tea for Two

As you may imagine, dear reader, I have many relations back home in New Zealand. They are liberally sprinkled over both North and South Islands and news of the success of *Malteser Merino* is slowly reaching Invercargill.

New Zealand can boast several famous authors: Katherine Mansfield, Samuel Butler, Thomas Bracken (who wrote the New Zealand national song), Dame Ngaio Marsh and W.H. Guthrie Smith who wrote *Tutira, The Story of a New Zealand Sheep Station*.

Dear Dame Ngaio and I once collaborated on a horror story, *The Canterbury Tail*. It is the account of a legendary flock of sheep whose mysterious disappearance and subsequent reappearance in the form of flying coathangers saved the town of Kaiapoi from Dastardly Desmond (an Australian, naturally) who wanted to build a Hollywood style Theme 'Park' in the middle of the Canterbury Plains. A TV miniseries of the book is planned and I have been asked to act as Executive Producer. Finding the right actors to play the ghostly flying sheep was not difficult... Near Te Kuiti in the North Island there is quite a large flock of my nephews and nieces. My great nephew Hipi would seem to be ideally cast as the hero of the piece.

Hipi flew over here recently for a holiday. Apparently Teddy Boy suits and shoulder pads are all the rage in downtown Auckland and Hipi was certainly a dedicated follower of fashion with shoulder pads and an outfit to out-glitter Gary Glitter. We had a day trip to Weston Super Mare. Hipi wore his new 'shades' and a denim jacket with 'I Love Kiri' embroidered on the back (bit of a clothes peg is our Hipi. He'd taken his Gucci swimming trunks and I had hoped to 'hang five' (in my old khaki shorts) on my surfboard but as usual the tide was out so we built sandcastles, rode on the train and strolled on the pier in search of 'Mr Gollivator World Pier Tour 1995' memorabilia. This keep-fit fanatic is quite the sensation of the South Coast... appearing 'twice nightly' in costumes that would out-Hipi Hipi.

When he arrived wearing a battered but trendy flying jacket, Hipi mistook Embers for a red lizard (snigger) which, of course, sent the Red Menace off in a right old huff! He huffed his way all down the garden and locked himself in the coal shed with a copy of *Hello* magazine.

Eventually he had to come in as we were going to see a friend of Hipi's (a New Zealand lady – his mentor, he says) who is in hospital. Embers was wearing his new floral bow tie in an effort to outshine Hipi who was in a fluorescent pink and blue zebra-striped casual shirt. I settled for something suitably casual but smart... something in which to be seen but not seen. My fountain pen was at the ready for the inevitable autograph. Embers had arranged a large bowl of red tulips as a gift for Kay, I took a small box of mint creams and Hipi took her a barrel of cider. (I tried to explain that Lucozade or Barley Water were traditional over here but he'd decided on cider and cider it would be!)

We found the ward, and Kay gave us a merry wave (a bit like a haka) of her walking stick as soon as she saw us. She was pleased to see Hipi (in his 'All Black' rugby shirt) and soon caught up on all the news of his starring role in *The Canterbury Tail*.

"See you've brought the red hippo," she said, poking her stick in Embers' direction as he appeared from behind his tulips. That did it! Back in an instant combustible huff he set fire to her 'Get Well Soon' cards: tulips flew everywhere and he bounced off the bed, knocking Sister's stethoscope from round her neck. It landed round his own. He strutted up and down the ward muttering to himself, and breathing fire and brimstone. Redder and redder he went (even his green bits). A group of student doctors arrived on the ward.

"Sir," said one, confusing him with Kay's consultant, "are we late for your round?"

Well, he puffed up his little red chest, twirled his stethoscope, straightened his bow-tie and cleared his throat. "Interesting case here," he said importantly. "Sheep who thinks he's a coat-hanger..."

Hipi, who was halfway through a bowl of Cape Grapes whilst reading *The Clothes Show* magazine, looked slightly bewildered, turned suddenly to say, "Who me?" and caught Embers on the back of his head with one of his (over) wide shoulder pads. Dr Dragon shot up in the air, somersaulted three times, grabbing Hipi as he went and they both landed on the tea trolley. It gathered speed down the ward, easily outpacing the stout tea-lady who had been settling an elderly lady with 'the cup that cheers'. They shot through the swing doors at the end of the ward, turned left through physiotherapy (collecting a crutch as they went) and out through outpatients where they had a passing encounter with a neatly folded pile of spare sheets and a small patient's toy telescope.

We could see them from the window, bumping through the car park, tea cups rattling, spoons jangling, on to the grass, pursued by the trolley's rightful steerer. Accelerating down the grassy bank... they spotted the River Yeo. Quick as a flash Embers stuck the crutch vertically into the tea urn, attached the sheet and 'SPLASH' they were launched. Somehow they were 'right sides up' but the current was strong and they were swept downstream, Embers shouting, "Splice the main brace!" and Hipi with the telescope humming *A Life On The Ocean Wave*. Both waved furiously as they went: we all waved back.

A seagull, name of Albert Ross, swooped overhead and followed them out to sea.

We had a postcard yesterday from Le Havre. Seems the Channel was a bit choppy but fortified by a few leftover cheese sandwiches and numerous cups of weak tea with ten sugar lumps... the Demon Dragon and his cabin boy have landed! They intend to travel on to La Flèche to spread a little 'entente cordiale' and to buy Hipi a Breton sweater and beret. He says he's grateful to Hipi for giving him the idea (?)... of staying on to race his tea trolley in the Le Mans 24-hour race. Vive Le Dragon Rouge!!

Bounce's Badminton Adventure

Badminton Bounce was, believe it or not, a donkey. He claimed, without any reliable documentation (unless you count a hoof print autograph) to be related to Red Rum. In his dreams, he had not only won the Grand National (several times) but the Derby, the Queen Mother Champion Chase ("Really," gasped an astonished Embers) and the four o'clock at Newton Abbot as well.

Early one morning he arrived with his brothers and sisters at Badminton House. The famous horse trials were to be held there that weekend. They were stabled in a cardboard box but by evening they were all smartly turned out on a stand in a marquee, their coats gleaming and their tails combed. Their owner, Mr Wilson, had disappeared into the village to the Fox and Hounds. Next day he would be very busy, the young visitors to the show loved his glove puppets.

For a while the toys played 'Guess the Badminton Winners'. They prided themselves on their knowledge of the event and Bounce could name ever winner since 1949! His brothers tested him. 1957? "High and Mighty ridden by Miss Sheila Wilcox,' he replied. 1984? "Easy-peasy – Beagle Bay."

But Bounce was bored...

He slid down from his shelf, peered under the marquee flap and decided a bit of exploring was just the thing for a spring evening...

His brothers Columbus, Killaire and Wattie scampered after him. Bounce was the youngest but he loved adventure.

They slipped between a row of huge horse boxes and into the show jumping ring. The bright colours of the fences, the triple bar, the oxer and the (ferocious) sharks-teeth planks dazzled them. The grass was so green, the fences so bright and the flags from all the different countries fluttered round the arena. Gaily striped marquees added to the kaleidoscope of colour.

Columbus, whose dapple grey coat shone in the evening sun, spotted the Royal Box and bowed low. "The winner will receive a great ovation when the Queen presents the cup," he said. "Perhaps she'll visit our stand and give us an apple each..." Columbus knew about royalty!

Killaire, a bright chestnut, had brought his Box Brownie camera and took photograph of them standing in front of a high five-bar gate. Wattie clambered up on a big red and white wall which was guarded by a row of conifer sentinels. "Look at me, I'm King William in his castle overlooking my Regal Realm! Take MY photograph, Killaire."

Bounce had seen the water jump and he wondered... "I wonder... if I could jump... SPLASH!

They formed a chain, holding each other's tails and held out a hoof to him. He shook himself dry. "That was priceless," laughed Wattie.

They dined on ice cream and delicious doughnuts and scampered off to the cross country course.

Soon they were jumping ditches at the Vicarage V, peering through the Shooting Butts at invisible poachers, and balancing on colossal rustic poles at Luckington Lane. They climbed up and down the Beaufort Staircase and nearly got lost in the maze of Tom Smith's walls.

"There are thirty fences on the course," said Columbus importantly, "and that fence over there is called the Cross Question."

"Why?" said the other donkeys – all together.

They came to the 'Lamb Creep'.

"I'd never get to sleep counting sheep jumping that," said Bounce, "it's too big. If I were a sheep, I'd go to sleep under it, nice and cosy under there. I like sheep. I'd like a sheep as a companion, a sheep would make a good chum, sheep are fun."

Wattie, Killaire and Columbus galloped round and round in circles.

"Now that could send me to sleep!" Bounce added.

They decided to investigate the lake and peered out from behind two trucks parked back to back to make sure no one was watching.

"This is the fence before the lake," Columbus informed them from on top of the shiny red truck filled with straw bales and flowers. "Tomorrow the horses will jump this.

"He's better than a guide book," whispered Killaire. "Come on let's paddle."

And gingerly they dipped their hooves into the water. Bounce decided that one bath a day was quite enough and sat in the evening sunshine on the upturned boat by the lake and thought some more about sheep.

"I would like a sheep as a friend, we could have lots of adventures and cuddle up together at night – save counting his relations."

"Did you know, went on Columbus, "that the game of badminton was invented in the big house over there?"

The others splashed him and fell about laughing on the grassy bank.

"Listen to him with his airs and graces," Killaire and Wattie giggled. "Come on Bounce, it's lovely and warm in the water – time you had a bath!" And they fell over in chuckling chaos and rolled down the slope back towards the lake.

"Hurry up, Mr Wilson's coming up the road past the kennels," said Bounce from his vantage point, and he slid off the boat to join his brothers.

"I'll take a quick photograph," said Killaire. "Everyone together, say 'apple pie'... One step back Bounce, I can't get you all in. One more step Bounce..." SPLASH!

The others scampered back, giggling giddily to the marquee. Bounce shook the water out of his ears.

At least he'd be nice and clean when he was purchased for the boy with the sheep tucked under his arm the next day... he didn't know it then but tomorrow he'd be sure... quite sure... the sheep winked at him!

Valerie Singleton, Where Are You?

Trips to London can be exhausting, but they can fire (sorry, Embers) the imagination. A wander down Drury Lane sets my mind racing with thoughts of *Malteser Merino*... Bonnie Langford, indeed!

Ernie decides that we should build a model of the set. He favours matchsticks and needless to say the Red Menace is all in favour of that. I point out that he'll probably burn the whole thing down unless we have Marguerite and the Weymouth Fire Brigade on standby while we glue, or he holds his breath for the duration of the project.

Russ, who is tinkering away on the old ivories (he's just written a little Italian sounding number called *La Chi Darem* which sounds vaguely Mozartian and familiar to someone used to playing the romantic lead) offers us a stack of old sardine tins for our model. We'll need some olive trees and a nice blue backdrop, surely sticky-backed plastic is the very thing! Nostalgic thoughts of Tracey Island!

Dispatch Ernie to Chippenham for supplies and go to look in the cupboard for Evostick – recalling a previous occasion when Embers appeared carrying a set of handlebars... and sneezed! In the resulting confusion, he slipped with the Evostick, some splashed on his head, the handlebars flew up in the air, sailed majestically

84

earthwards... and got stuck between his ears... talk about Rudolph the Red Nosed Dragon...

At this very moment the phone rings, it's Elizabeth (Elizabeth who?). Playing for time I enquire after her health – "We are well," she replies.

The penny drops (heads! Elizabeth) and I bow graciously, or as graciously as one can when holding a half-empty can of Evostick. "Could we speak to Mr Dragon?..."

"He's a tad busy... could I take a message?"

"Mother would like him to know that she is free for drinks on the 30th, profuse apologies for not attending the fête" (fête indeed) "but she was detained by a large Australian lady who'd mislaid some raffle tickets during the last race at Ascot. The Australian was so distraught, she just knew she'd won a prize, that Mother had felt obliged to invite her to Windsor to tea." ("There's a nice little tea shop opposite the Castle," Elizabeth confided.)

Elizabeth then asked "to whom was one speaking" and I gave my name. "Not THE Hadlee Sheep?"

"The very same," I confessed.

I suppose it's the result of fame, 'one' has to accept it and before I can say 'mint sauce' the lady is asking for "just a teensy weeny part in your play, Mr Sheep?"

"We would be delighted, Ma-am," I replied... I could almost feel the sword on my shoulder: 'Arise, Sir Hadlee Sheep'.

I bow again, replace the receiver, and go in search of Embers who is now firmly attached to the 'on' switch on the television.

He just had to see what his namesake was up to in the cricket. I had a quick look myself, just to make sure that that Boycott chap hadn't got a game as well when the phone rang again and luckily I pretended to be the answerphone. I say luckily because 'after the tone' is the voice of a very irate Michael Ball who has been offered the part of Tal Bonc the singing greengrocer in our production. Well, I thought it was ideal casting but, it seems, Mr Ball thinks he can do better as Hadlee Sheep. (I reckon he'd be a touch too wooden as an olive tree).

Next thing we know he'll be volunteering his services for fete-opening.

That reminds me, I must catch up with my post. There is a very elegant letter from someone signing herself 'Diana' who wants to audition for a clothes horse (and I didn't even know we had one)... and dear old Richard Branson, the sweetie, can't remember why I had to write, but I'm sure he'd appreciate a letter and I could remind him about the Jumbo Jet. Embers has had no luck finding one in his Argos catalogue... Virgin must have a spare one.

A knock on the door.

Don't touch... too late... the handle Embers.

My, my, it's little Johnny Herbert who last Sunday won the British Grand Prix. What a star! I wrote to congratulate him and apologise for Embers pedalling past him on his lap of honour. And waving with BOTH hands, Johnny, no wonder we're fans of yours – something for the dragon to practise on his bike!

We asked Johnny to pop in if he was passing... and he has. With his help I free Embers only to find that Johnny is now attached to the door handle – a novel way of steering a Formula 1 car... well done Johnny.

Having caused havoc with his trolley in Sainsbury's, Ernie returns with enough sticky-backed plastic for three Tracey Islands, washing up liquid, loo rolls and a few cardboard boxes.   What fun this will be.   We invite Johnny to join us and use his helmet to soak the papier mâché... I wonder whatever became of Valerie Singleton and that nice little elephant?

The Dragon Looks Sweet

Embers is busy: he has his bicycle in pieces in the middle of the sitting room. In fact he has two bicycles in pieces... the second one is a tricycle that used to belong to the Young Master. From a safe distance a sheep can only wonder what the Red Menace is trying to achieve...

He is wearing a very snazzy pair of red and green striped overalls, his tail tucked neatly into the back pocket. Since his little accident with the handlebars and the Evostick, he's been very safely conscious, and even carries a pocket fire extinguisher for that 'unexpected (dragon) emergency'. Firefighter Newman would be proud of him.

He is humming softly to himself: *Cwym Rhondda*, and (I do declare) *Rule Britannia* and it's not even the Last Night of the Proms. He did casually mention that anything Bryn Terfel could do he could probably do better, after I intimated that I thought Mr Terfel might like to audition (along with Michael Ball) for the part of 'Tal Bonc' the singing greengrocer in *Malteser Merino*. I suppose (with a suitable false beard, gold tooth and hooped earring, the Red Menace could do it, but I'm not too confident about him juggling all those oranges whilst balancing a watermelon on his head.

Anyway, all *sotto voce* and emotional he moves on to *Jerusalem*, gets to the bit about clouds unfolding and bringing him a chariot of fire... when up he jumps: he's got it, he announces...

"Got what?" I venture to ask just a tad warily. "The cure for the common cold? The lottery jackpot ticket?"

("The winner of the 2.30 at Newmarket?" chips in Bounce.)

No... the name of his new bicycle. *The Red Rover*.

His creation, using two large wheels (with a steering handle attached to each) and one smaller rear wheel, is just perfect for climbing hills (he says), perfectly safe for a 'lady' and very comfortable. He tightens a last bolt and promptly hops on it and disappears up our hill singing at the top of his little Welsh voice.

We begin to wonder if he has disappeared in the Studley Triangle, but no, in the distance, someone is singing: "...In the good old summertime... Don't sit under the apple tree, with anyone else but me, oh, no, no..." and "Ain't she sweet... I ask you very confidentially..."

Embers has changed: he is wearing plus-fours, a bowler hat and a false moustache. Soon he is whizzing back down the hill waving and doffing his hat with his tail. He dismounts (from the rear) at a good ten miles an hour, bows to us, and the bicycle careers on down the hill, gathering speed and narrowly missing the signpost on the bridge where it slithers to a halt by the old railway gate. Embers scratches his little red head and scampers off down the hill to rescue his contraption.

Three drawing books later he has another idea: *The Dragonara*. "Much more suitable for a lady," he says, as he tinkers away happily, a small photograph of his 'heart's desire' propped up against a spare pedal. Bounce and Hayzee decide to take *The Red Rover* out for a test drive and operate one steering handle (and one pedal) each. They decide, for safety's sake, to ride round Farmer Harding's field and have been gone some time when I myself take my trusty boneshaker out for a spin.

They were heading for the cornfield, it appears, when something snapped and Hayzee's steering malfunctioned. They arrived at the open gateway, hit a large stone and hurtled into space, landing safely ("proving something," said the Red Menace) in the middle of the ripening wheat. They had been proceeding round and round in a labyrinthine, roundabout route for some time before hitting another stone and being catapulted back towards the farmhouse. Mr Harding, looking out of an upstairs window, spotted the phenomenon but not the bicyclists, telephoned the *News of the World* and thus the 'corn circle' was invented.

I found my cronies sitting by the roadside: Hayzee wearing the bowler hat at a rather unique angle and Bounce upside down in the ditch muttering something about 'Dragons not being safe as pets' and 'St George was his favourite saint'.

I digress. Embers, back at 'Chez Sheep', was working wonders with his *Dragonara*. He was humming 'Daisy Daisy' and, clever old sheep that I am, I deduced his velocipede was to be a tandem. He would drive and his 'heart's desire' would ride (majestically) behind. The basket on the front was lined with a small tartan blanket (suitable for carrying a small dog, should 'one' wish, explained a rather excitable dragon). The saddle bag contained a picnic hamper, another tartan blanket, a portable gramophone, a tin of dog biscuits, a slim volume

on corgis and a small silver bowl marked 'Aquarius'. On the handlebars a Royal Standard pennant was unfurled.

Sunday morning: Embers has been up all night, repositioning and realigning, oiling and polishing. He had made cucumber sandwiches and baked tiny pasties and pies for the picnic basket. A bottle of (Welsh) champagne and another of his own recipe Parsnip Wine were chilling.

"The *Dragonara* is ready," he announced, and whisked off one of the Young Master's sheets to reveal his masterpiece. On the rear seat was a posy of spring flowers tied with a ribbon. Attached to the handle-bars of his 'bicycle made for two' was a red, white and blue ribbon and a card 'To Elizabeth, with love from your most ardent admirer and loyal subject, Embers the Dragon'.

He hopped into his plus-fours, put a daffodil in his button-hole, threw his tail jauntily over his left shoulder, turned on his mobile phone and pedalled off 'solo' to collect his date.

"Elizabeth said it was either a picnic with me or listen to Kiri Te Kanawa on the radio," he explained... no contest... she said the Dame could put a sock in it... I've sent Kiri one of mine. The Fair Isle red and green one with the hole in the toe.

Not Very Natural and Almost History

I suppose if one consorts with dragons one should be accustomed to heat. This summer it has been hot! Sitting around the bird bath one morning, dipping the occasional toe whilst sipping a glass of mint tea, Russ scampered up the path with the post. Listen to one who knows, sardine-flavoured post is unacceptable. A seal wallowing in one's bird bath is nearly as bad!

As usual, all the most interesting letters were for his Dragonship. True, I had a '10 pence off' voucher for the new Persil – all action, remove every known stain and some you'd rather not know about – washing powder, and my library book was ready for collection, *Righting the Wrongs in your Writing* – a handbook for the experienced novelist, and I had a letter (pink paper, naturally) from Miss Cartland (she'd previously asked me to star as her next romantic hero in a book tipped to be a Hollywood blockbuster), thanking me for my suggestions. (1. Change the spelling of your name – 'Baabaara' has more of a ring, don't you think? Streisand tried it, didn't get it quite right... but she's done well for herself, nevertheless.)

Embers has a formal letter with a South London postmark: "Dear Mr Dragon, as you may have read in the press, our new extension has been fully refurbished and we are seeking a celebrity of your stature [snigger] to perform the opening ceremony. I have pleasure in enclosing second class omnibus tickets for you, your friend Mr Sheep and your 'minder' and look forward to greeting you at the museum for our champagne launch on August 10th." Well, I'll go to the foot of our stairs.

Off he goes strutting around the garden, polishing his fete opening scissors, practising his bow, falling in the fish pond. (well, if we had one he'd fall in it – just a little artistic licence here by yours sheepishly). But which museum, Embers? I sneaked a look at the letter... and read on...

"You and your companion will make a magnificent display alongside Mick the Miller, Chi Chi the giant panda, Shergar (not many people know that!) and our world famous diplodocus 'Bony-parts'..." Actually that's my little joke, but don't tell the dragon, he had himself positioned right alongside the Komodo dragon... till I sniggered and gave the game away.

We did have bus tickets to London and we did take the Young Master, it was his birthday the next day and we thought he was in need of a treat. The wheels on the bus went round and round and we looked for a game to play. 'Spot the haystack' has limited possibilities and I've never been one for counting sheep. So 'community singing' it was. *Puff the Magic Dragon* seemed a bit tricky for some of the older passengers. Embers suggested *London's Burning* as a round and the Young Master said he'd prefer a round of cheese and pickle sandwiches. We decided on a medley of wartime favourites: *We'll Meet Again*, *Pack Up Your Troubles*, *It's A Long Way To Tipp-a-Dragon* and when we got to *The White Cliffs of Dover* the driver stopped the bus and said if we wanted Dover we should have caught the Dover bus (and hopefully the ferry – that's an idea!) and left him in peace... What a mint sauce. And after Embers had given him that copy of the Highway Code too...

Victoria to Kensington: the bus or the underground? Tricky when you're nine inches tall, so we hopped into the Young Master's rucksack, with the football magazines, the lists of players, the soccer cards and the FA quiz book, and hitched a lift.

All very interesting, we saw the Komodo dragon before it saw Embers. "Was that why it was smiling?" he whispered. "Thinks HE's the only proper dragon in the world! Doesn't say much, does he?" (Probably couldn't get word in – Embers rattled on and on... "What's that snake? Hello Monty, are you a python?"

We looked at the birds, the reptiles, the fish and the human beings... A huge blue whale swam in the mid air in the 'Mammal Hall'. I looked round and Embers had disappeared. Then I saw him sitting on the whale's tail, waving. The attendant seemed to wave back then shook his fist, Embers waved again and the attendant said he was a 'hooligan' and shouldn't have been allowed in.

I can only say that the new Dinosaur exhibition was opened by a true 'exhibitionist'. For effect, he perched a pair of spectacles on the end of his nose. He invited the gathered dignitaries to wander round with him, he marvelled at the megalosaurus, was intrigued by the iguanadon, stunned by the stegosaurus and reduced to a quivering wreck by Tyrannosaurus 'Rex' himself.

"Perhaps you know my friend the Queen Mother?" he inquired in a faltering voice, scampering backwards away from the (very) accurate lifesize model, teeth included... "She'll have you in the Tower for this, mark my words."

As he retreated another pace he backed into brontosaurus, causing a collision with compsognathus and gallimimus. Bones flew everywhere, the curator was in tears, I caught a passing leptoceratops' leg and rushed for the exit, dismissing the idea of a souvenir keyring from the shop. As the security men gathered round the Red Menace he pulled a tube of 'UHU' from his pocket covered in fluff, bits of old bus ticket and discarded sweet papers – the top had come off.

"Perhaps this might help," he suggested...

Another fine mess.

The bus home. The same driver – false beard and disguise, quick. This time we'd sing the 'Okie Cokie' knees bend arms stretch, baah, baah, baah. The Young Master, the passengers and I, that is. Embers – he'd been kept in as the star attraction of the Natural History Museum.

Howdy, Squiggles!

Embers has an idea (he has lots of them). This one is for a self-igniting barbecue! Just the thing for those sultry summer evenings. Friends pop round. Drink? Lovely. Mint julep... long and cold. Peckish? Let's light the barbecue and sizzle a sausage. Job done, no fuss, in bed by nine with a good book.

I suggest we wait until May, but, no, the Red Menace wants a demonstration on January 18th. Barbecue weather in New Zealand perhaps...

So it's out with the muffler, the thermal vest and two pairs (four in my case) of nice woolly socks. We troop off down the garden, at least he has the good grace to supply us with a mug of cocoa each. Embers is doing it in style. Not only does he have the best plastic plates from Mr Sainsbury's shelves, gleaming plastic cutlery and sparkling crystal plastic tumblers, but, he has decorated the table with a linen cloth, napkins and a vase of fresh winter jasmine.

Imagine, if you will, the scene. With one flick of a switch the barbecue is glowing. Our lunch guest, none other than Mr Gollivator – "do call me Gilbert" – is relaxing on the sun-lounger tapping a little black finger to his latest routine which he is playing on his 'Walkman'.

Ernie is busy slicing rolls for the hotdogs, ketchup everywhere, and I am busy reading a letter from Cameron

Mackintosh who thinks Sooty might be the very person to star in *Malteser Merino*! Sooty!!! (There's always a bear, lurking, ready to dance his way into a person's best musical – even if he is legless.) Think again, Mr Mackintosh, or its me and Sir Andrew from here on in.

The frost is thawing from my reading glasses, the ice has nearly all melted in the bird bath and Embers is whistling to himself as he cooks, green scales peeping out from his jauntily set chef's hat, little blue and white striped apron round his little red stomach, his tail thrown casually over his left shoulder, in case he should turn suddenly and singe it.

Our very own Delia Smith is about to serve a 'culinary triumph' (his words), his recipes are his own and the cookery book is only used to prop up a rather unstable table.

From up in the clouds we hear a distant rumble, ("Thunder, or my stomach rumbling," declares Gilbert from behind his designer shades) which, as it gets closer sounds more like the spluttering of an engine. Suddenly from behind the third fluffy nimbus on the left comes a tiny speck of a biplane. It rolls, it dives, it loops the loop and we gaze up – transfixed. Embers' tail slithers off his shoulder and lands on the barbecue, we sit him in the water butt as the plane lands on the lawn. Out of it swaggers a small, amber-furred figure – Sooty? – (surely not) complete with sheepskin jacket (mint sauce) red neckerchief, flying helmet and goggles (silk scarf and underwear at the cleaners, he explained later).

Biggles? No, 'Squiggles' says "Howdy y'all" and introduces himself to Embers who has now recovered his equilibrium (although not his hat) and is staring fork tongued at our unannounced guest.

"This is my aeroplane, 'Liberty Belle'" he announces with a flourish and a slight Texan drawl. "'WE' are at the service of Dragonair, saw your advertisement. Consider the post of 'co-pilot' filled by yours truly." And with that he sat down, helped himself to a sausage, and put his booted feet up on the table.

Despite his rather cocksure arrival (and being a bear) he's a likeable fellow, seems to have spent some time (years even) wandering round Heathrow trying to clear immigration. Then some kindly member of staff found him dozing on a shelf, pointed out our advertisement, wound his propeller and sent him down to us.

He helps himself to a large bourbon (biscuit) and tells us about 'back home in Texas'. There's 266,807 miles of it and he covers every inch.

"Ever been down Sesame Street?" asks Ernie.

He tells us of Pecan trees (state tree), and Mockingbirds (state bird) and Bluebonnets (state flower). Sings us a chorus or five of *Texas, our Texas* and tells us the state motto is 'Friendship'. Sounds like he's read it all on the Young Master's Texas T-shirt.

"I think he's from Hounslow or Hammersmith," mutters Gilbert, resplendent in a striped blazer, with a yawn. Just as the sun is beginning to shed its watery winter light on our little picnic, and Embers is serving the 'crêpes Suzette' (flambéed, naturellement), a shadow passes over the patio. Something hard lands right between my ears; I see stars, Bonnie Langford, Paddington Bear, Michael Ball... Sooty, and go a little giddy.

I look upwards, and high above us, breathing fire (Embers is in love) is a hot-air balloon, with what looks like 'Virgin' inscribed on it. Waving furiously from the basket is a bearded person in the finest, fancy Fair Isle.

Another blast of hot air (this time from Embers) and the balloon is away towards the River Avon.

"Funny thing to write on a balloon," queries Squiggles, now on his third crepe and fourth bourbon, as I cast my eyes downwards and notice at my feet a house brick; attached to it is a letter addressed to 'Mr Hadlee Sheep, Managing Director: Dragonair... by air'. It's a takeover bid, Richard Branson wants to take over Dragonair. Embers is hopping mad, hop, hop, hop he goes all round the bird-bath.

"Let me see that," says Squiggles, reaching out for the letter which he reads quickly, crumples and tosses over his shoulder. He sprints back to 'Liberty Belle' winds his propeller, springs into the cockpit, shouting something like 'bandits four o'clock high' (which wakes Gilbert who mutters "that time already – I'll take my nap") and in a cloud of smoke he's off after the balloon and buzzes it all the way round the M25 and down to Dover... decent chap 'Squiggles'... the exemption that proves the rule concerning BEARS!

Celebration!

Thursday morning: the kitchen was such a hive of activity that the Young Master's mum announced "I'm going to school and the Post Office and I want this mess" (mint sauce, we're 'creating') "cleared up by the time I return."

Allow me to explain: a few days' later there was to be a celebration. A festival of revelry. Bounce was busy with pen and paper writing invitations. Being a donkey, writing was not and still isn't his best subject and all his 'mistooks' were scrunched up and tossed nonchalantly over his left shoulder. Mess?... no.

Squiggles was oiling Liberty Belle's engine, whether the kitchen floor was the best place for this task was, I must agree, debatable.

Hayzee was making a 'corn dolly' as a gift. He says it's a neglected rural craft and as a New Forest pony it is his duty to revive the art. Some might not agree and neither would the NSPCCD (the National Society for the Prevention of Cruelty to Corn Dollies). Surplus straw can be a problem.

Moley was looking things up in his encyclopedia whilst chewing a bag of toffees.

Russ was arranging a 'variation on the theme of a well loved tune'.

Edward was making sausage rolls, 'just like the ones they serve in Southampton.' And washing up. "But does Southampton washing up have all those suds, Edward?" Empty washing up liquid bottle? Never mind!

Runcie was in charge of 'dessert' – banana splits, banana ice cream and banana whirls. Okay a few banana skins had hit the floor, a tad slippery but mess?... no.

Squirry was decorating the patio with fairy lights, needless to say, in the best of Christmas traditions, they would not work and he had them festooned round the kitchen – searching for the non-working culprit.

Ernie was blowing up balloons whilst watching a video of Sesame Street and singing along to the *Rubber Duck*-song: not easy with balloons.

And then we have Embers. He'd just returned from the village hall. The WI invited him to judge their 'decorated bicycle' competition. Much to her delight, Mrs Hutchings had won six tickets to see Sooty in pantomime!

"I'll take my grandchildren," she told Embers... "Perhaps you and Mr Sheep would like to join us?"

Inexplicably the village hall curtains spontaneously combusted. Embers pedalled home as fast as his little red legs would go.

Having removed his bicycle clips and slung his tail over his shoulder in his usual casual fashion, he decided to make a start on the cake.

He mixed it, he whisked it, and he gave it an hour on Gas Mark 4. Our own little Delia Smith then turned it upside down and removed the middle (creating a plate of fairy cakes as he went!). He iced his confection in red and green (adding a few sugar daffodils for effect), ready to climb inside it, (igniting the candles as he went) and jump out five minutes later shouting, 'surprise'.

Myself, my artistic streak is well known. I had designed a card. It was a tad (mint) saucy but I threw caution to the wind for this special occasion.

Gilbert, 'Mr Gollivator' telephoned to say he would be delighted to accept our invitation and would arrive at three. Was it true that our guest of honour was a fan of *Star Trek*? He had just the gift... a pair of Mr Spock ears!

I admit a small amount of glue did attach itself to the telephone – not enough to be described as 'a mess' and a few of the stars from the gift wrap got stuck to it – it looked very pretty.

Card finished, I made a banner to fly behind 'Liberty Belle'.

But would we have all our tasks finished before the return of the Young Master's mum?... Would she notice the, um... mess?

As you know, we are avid *Blue Peter* viewers: Tracey Island was no problem to us. We reviewed the situation. We had a pile of toffee papers, some scrunched-up paper, flour, water, icing sugar, food colouring and the odd banana skin. A pile of straw, paints (and Bounce's tail for a brush) and some engine oil. Okay the glue was in short supply as most of it was attached to the phone, but we'd manage.

Footsteps on the path: quick as a (red) flash we built a model of the Starship Enterprise, gift wrapped it in star spangled paper and attached the card. Ernie stood by with dustpan and brush... Mess? What mess? No mess... Let us make you a nice cup of tea.

The next day on the patio, fairy lights twinkled, Russ was ready in his tails with Mrs Webb (and a candelabra) at the piano, our guests arrived: Millie Molly Manley and her Milestones, the Vicar with the Headmaster and Mr Birch.

Also from school, Mrs Jennings and Mrs Parker who recklessly sampled Embers' Parsnip wine, while Misses Kimber, Beresford and Wackett pondered over the 'Ferret's Favourite'. Mrs Wheelwright had been 'held up' by Chris Hunt and Year Four.

The Village Postmaster and his lady wife arrived with our jolly postman and a small person in wellingtons and a floppy hat "I didn't invite him" whispers Bounce just as our guest of honour arrived on the arm of 'Mr Gollivator'...

Squiggles took off and flew over Studley... Happy Birthday, Miss Tarragon!

Postscript

Saturday: I'm beginning to dread the jolly postman's even jollier whistle. With his cheery 'good morning', Persil coupons and tips for the second race at Sandown Park... you never know what's going to happen next! The strangest things have been posted through our letter box (eg Russ: I rest my case).

Today a letter marked 'Selfridges'. Would Mr Dragon be free to run Santa's Grotto this December. They felt (the Royal Ballet had agreed) that his tap dancing Rudolf the Red Nosed Reindeer act would be just the thing to entertain the children waiting to see good old F.C. (ho, ho, ho!)

Whilst HE is thinking about it, I write a quick line back saying that we do a nice line in elves and 'woodland folk', the Andrews Sisters aren't doing much early December and could entertain over afternoon tea and I could fit in a book signing session if I practise the flourish on my signature.

Second letter: Cameron Macintosh asking him to audition for HIS smash hit new musical. And he's heard rumours of a new production, *Dragon Rampant*, the story of a famous aviator who never quite took off (snigger). Mr Macintosh says it has possibilities (mint sauce).

Third letter: the Bumpkin Boffins want him to be their lead singer. He's always fancied himself as Gary Glitter and his jitterbug is nearly as remarkable as his tap dancing.

Mr Gollivator has suggested a 'world tour'... and Mrs Webb would very much like to be HIS full-time pianist and Mrs Jennings would be delighted to handle his fan mail. What fan mail? My fan mail, perhaps!

He's had pantomime offers too: Buttons in *Cinderella* and the Prince in *Sleeping Beauty*. Pantomime is rather more the Dragon's style but whatever he does I think we'll have to ask Dame Joan or Millie Molly Manley to tune him up a bit first... and his name has been suggested for a 'cameo' role in *Star Trek – Beyond the Realms of Fantasy*.

He's doing celebrity 'talks' at local coffee mornings, demonstrating his patented self-igniting barbecue at the WI, visiting the bewildered at the Old Folks home and the Vicar still wants him to open the refurbished church tower... if it involves a speech, cutting ceremonial ribbons or kissing babies, he's sure to say 'yes'.

He's been out with the Vicar this morning, cycling round the village on his *Dragonara* (Mk 2), wearing his Tour de France medal and waving to his fans.

But he's waited in vain for days for his invitation to his friend Elizabeth's Jubilee jamboree. He's made her a card (featuring a picture of himself waving) and is, as I write, making her a special cake in the shape of a crown. He's covered in chocolate from nose to tail, and has eaten all the glacé cherries but if we stick a candle on his head he can be his own singing cake-o-gram! And, he won't need a box of Swan Vestas...

Meanwhile, myself, I've had enough adventure, I'm taking it easy... I'll look through the manuscript of *Dragon Rampant*, have a chat with Sir Andrew about its musical possibilities and ask Dame Heidi to choreograph it. Then I'll curl up with a good book (hopefully not written by or starring a bear) and dream of days past, full of adventure, of bus rides and cricket, of fêtes, and holidays and of *Malteser Merino*.